THEY HEARD THE TELLTALE DRONING
OF POWERFUL ENGINES

Then the Zeros swarmed out of the sky, guns blazing and chattering out a grim song of vengeance. Private Tommy Wyszynski fired at the oncoming plane, and he saw the incandescent tracer rounds spray up into the sky and a couple of rounds strike the Zero's wings.

But the Zero kept on coming straight for him, and he seemed frozen in place. Suddenly flame belched from the machine-gun ports located at the front of the Japanese attack plane, and the GI's moment of truth came in a terrible burst of heat and light and sound.

Sergeant Scully was standing with his legs splayed, his tommy gun's buttstock jammed against his shoulder blade. Twin lines of bullets kicked up clods of mud and pulverized rock as the pilot now triggered his forward guns at the American below.

"Come a little closer!" Scully shouted between clenched teeth. Then the Zero was dead on him, and Scully opened up with the stuttering tommy gun.

CALIFORNIA

SOLDIERS OF WAR

TIDE OF VICTORY
William Reed

A GOLD EAGLE BOOK FROM
WORLDWIDE ®

TORONTO • NEW YORK • LONDON • PARIS
AMSTERDAM • STOCKHOLM • HAMBURG
ATHENS • MILAN • TOKYO • SYDNEY

This book is dedicated to the fighting men of the 40th Infantry Division, and especially those of the 160th Infantry Regiment. May our nation never allow their exploits in the Pacific theater of war to fade from memory. It is also dedicated to Filipino war veterans who served courageously in and alongside the United States military, and who have only recently been accorded full acknowledgment of their contribution to America's war effort in the Pacific.

This is a work of fiction, loosely and broadly based on the campaign in Luzon, the Philippines. Except in the case of major historical figures and events, this book makes no attempt whatsoever to portray actual persons and situations or to document occurrences. It is purely and completely a work of the imagination.

First edition November 1991

ISBN 0-373-63403-X

Special thanks and acknowledgment to
David Alexander for his contribution to this work.

TIDE OF VICTORY

AUTHOR'S NOTE

The battle for the Philippine Islands centered on Luzon. Because the island is roughly equal in size to the British Isles, nowhere in the Pacific theater could land-based troops of division strength wage war on the scale of European engagements. Indeed, the battle for Luzon involved the second-largest American troop commitment of the entire war, save that which followed the D-Day invasion landings in Normandy, France.

Commanded by General Tomoyuki Yamashita, the Japanese forces on Luzon were thinly stretched. Knowing that an assault formation of American combat troops was coming, General Yamashita concentrated his forces in three strategic locations. The first stronghold was the vast mountain wilderness to the north of the island, the second was the heights east of Manila, and the third was the rough mountain country of the Bataan Peninsula. In these places men fought some of the fiercest battles of World War II.

Despite all of this, ultimate defeat was a certainty for the Japanese. Since the Japanese usually chose death before surrender, the only question left was precisely when the inevitable defeat would occur. It turned out that the Japanese were not fully evicted from Luzon until the very end of the war, and indeed, reports of holdouts in the wilds of the northern part of the island continued to filter in until well after the war was over.

BOOK ONE:
The Dying Place

1

It was a hill without a name. Only a number.

The men of Blackjack Company were ordered to take it, and they were determined to do it or die in the attempt.

The place had a name. *Luzon*. A big rock in the Philippine Islands complex pushed upward out of the ocean's depths by the earth's birth pangs in the prehistoric past, its mountain highlands covered with jungle.

Luzon. An island teeming with Japanese forces, a giant stepping-stone in the broad expanse of the Pacific toward Tokyo. General Douglas MacArthur, head of the U.S. Army in the Far East, was tasked with the prosecution of the war in this Pacific combat theater.

The Amphtracs that had ferried Company B to shore from the U.S. troop carrier anchored in the choppy waters of the South China Sea were long gone, either blown up by shelling or safely back from where they had come. Beyond the beach were groves of bamboo and isolated stands of wild coconut palms and fields of parched brown *kunai* grass and brakes of native sugarcane.

And then began the heights.

MASTER SERGEANT Matt Scully, one of the first off
the sea-land Amphtracs, clutched his Thompson submachine gun, outfitted with a drum magazine
crammed to full capacity with .45-caliber ammunition, and signaled the all-clear to Third Platoon.
Scully was a former boxer, his face a mute testimony
to his pugilistic past. His gravelly voice suggested bar-
room brawls and too many nights of drinking gin.

Third Platoon was dug in behind Scully in the hollows of the fine-grained volcanic sands, taking shelter
behind big rocks and fallen trees knocked down by violent tropical squalls.

"Move out!" he shouted. "Come on! Get the lead
out of your butts. This is no cakewalk. This is a war,
dammit!"

Scully's gruff voice was full of bravado, but his
flinty gray eyes spoke another language entirely. Those
eyes were keen and burned with a combat veteran's
innate sense of caution, scanning the terrain to the
front and the rear and the cloudless blue sky above for
signs of danger.

Corporal Eddie Mockler came loping up behind the
sergeant. Of average height, Mockler had a three-day
beard and a blank expression on his face. But the eyes
betrayed the truth, for they were fully alert in the
haggard face. Like Scully, Mockler was outfitted with
the khaki fatigues, helmet and combat boots of a
fighting soldier in the Pacific theater of operations.

Both Scully and Mockler wore the diamond-shaped
patch of the Fortieth Infantry Division emblazoned on

the shoulder, a patch depicting the golden disk of the sun with twelve pointed rays extending against a background of deep blue.

The Fortieth was called the Sunshine Division and it was attached to the California National Guard. Blackjack Company was attached to the 160th Infantry Regiment. It was a unit whose personnel were recruited largely from the Los Angeles area.

Some attributed B-Company's name to the card game, others to the makeshift saps filled with lead buckshot that supposedly a former commander had carried and that many of the men still did as a regular part of their gear.

The khaki fatigues of Third Platoon were much the same as those worn by GIs serving in Italy or France. In addition to the helmets covered with the familiar netting, the men carried long knives scabbarded at their waists or slung on their backs within easy reach. Those knives would allow them to hack their way through the dense underbrush of the rain-forested volcanic islands.

The knives were also useful for close-quarter combat against the Japanese, who were notorious for their deadly samurai swords as well as the bayonets attached to their rifles. The Japanese had a taste for engaging in hand-to-hand battle. That was a preference not shared by their German or Italian counterparts, nor, for that matter, their American opponents. In Europe combatants had been known to throw stones at each other when their ammunition ran out rather than resort to hand-to-hand combat.

The men who landed on Luzon were different from the earlier wave of GIs, too. They were of a different caliber than the troops the Japanese had chased from Bataan and Corregidor approximately two years before. These troops were better trained and equipped, and more determined than ever to win back the Pacific for America and make the enemy pay for Pearl Harbor.

Now, in the war's concluding months, they had completed the evolution of the American fighting man into its final product. They were *professionals,* men who no longer thought of peace or of the loved ones they had left behind, men who no longer even thought of life or death. Their only thought was to push on toward the next objective and the next one after that, on and on until the day when the war had finally been won—by their side.

"You think the Japs seen us yet?" Mockler began. "They must have spotted us already. Why ain't they shooting yet?"

"The Japs heard you were coming," Scully rasped. "They heard what a crackerjack you were. They're waiting to see your stuff. I bet they even baked you a cake."

"I don't care what you say. I know they are watching us right now. You know how I know it?"

"Because your knuckles itch," Scully answered from the side of his mouth, having heard the routine before.

"That's right," Mockler answered, scratching his right hand. "My knuckles always itch when there's Japs around. It never fails. I even told the doc about it once. You know what he told me, Sarge?"

"He said you were nutty as a fruitcake," Scully said, keeping his eyes trained on the edge of the jungle ahead of them. He didn't want to admit it, but the hairs on his neck were behaving in exactly the same way that Mockler's knuckles were.

"That's right, Sarge. He did. But you know what I say to that? I say the sawbones is crazy. I say they're *all* crazy. I know what I know, and when my knuckles itch, there's Jap in the vicinity."

Farther down the GI line, Privates Jacek and Trouty were also getting a creepy feeling. Jacek was a dance hall romeo from Los Angeles. In the ballrooms back home in L.A., he cut a mean number with his girlfriend and dance partner Annabell. Jacek had big plans for himself when the war was over and done with. He and Annabell were going to become the hottest dance sensation since Fred Astaire and Ginger Rogers.

Trouty came from Culver City and had entertained less extravagant hopes of managing a burger joint before he was drafted into the service. He had only vague notions of using his demobilization pay to start either a swank gambling casino or a first-class hook shop. At this point he didn't know which, but he was working on figuring it out.

"I'll lay you odds the Jap is watching us right now," Jacek said to Trouty. He clutched the Browning Automatic Rifle in his hands tightly, as though the rifle were a magic talisman and gave him some guarantee of survival against the long odds of the war.

"They say the Jap won't surrender," Trouty put in, thinking of the kind of women he'd have in his hook shop. Round, firm and fully packed. That was the ticket. Dames who were stacked like Jane Russell and Anne Sheridan. Dames with plenty of moxie and oomph. "They say the Jap cuts the heads off the enemy for fun. You hear that dope, Jacek?"

"I hear a lot of scuttlebutt, Trouty," Jacek returned. "Most of it is strictly for the birds."

Trouty started to say something, but all that came out of his mouth was a bright shower of blood. Jacek heard the crack of the bullet a moment later, just as Trouty collapsed to the sand in a crumpled heap. Now Jacek was hearing more shots.

He dodged quickly for cover just as the canopy of palms erupted with a chorus of chattering gunfire. Snipers up in the palms of the trees were firing down on the platoon. His company's CO had told the men just before landing that the enemy had the habit of tying themselves into the trees with vines and even letting themselves hang there, playing possum, hoping to shoot a guy in the back that way.

Well, this sniper wasn't getting a second chance to put a bullet into an American's back. "You dirty, rotten Nip!" Jacek hollered as he aimed the BAR up and got off a long burst of .30-caliber bullets, the first of them glowing like hot rivets as they sailed skyward because he had loaded tracer rounds at the top of the clip.

Whether through luck or skill or a combination of both, the first few rounds of the burst scored perfect bull's-eyes. The sniper's head exploded, and he crashed down from the canopy amid the clatter of splintering tree branches.

The sniper's left boot was tied to a vine, which pulled taut as he fell. Instead of hitting the ground, he went crashing into the trunk of the tree, shaking loose a bunch of green coconuts in the process. Rebounding, the dead soldier kept swinging back and forth on the end of the vine.

All along the beach, the men of Third Platoon were returning fire at the enemy. The soldiers of the Sunshine Division had arrived at their destination.

They had come to the dying place.

2

"Gotcha, sir," Scully said into the mouthpiece of the walkie-talkie, and handed the unit to the platoon's radioman, Sparks Watkins. He'd just been talking to Blackjack Company's commander, Lieutenant Bloodworth, who had set up a temporary command post located just a little inland from one of the landing zone's other beaches.

Bloodworth's orders were to proceed toward the heights and secure their northern flank. Some elements of the company had already engaged the enemy in the vicinity and reported that the area was a veritable hornets' nest of bunkers and gun emplacements set into the mouths of natural limestone caverns. It was a killing ground where the Japanese could crawl through the fields of man-high *kunai* grass, finish off their victims then move on to the next target.

The rest of the troops of Third Platoon were dug in here and there along the sand at the periphery of the palm grove where they had halted, taking cover behind fallen logs, tree trunks, boulder outcroppings and whatever shelter the landscape afforded.

Most of the platoon was holed up inside the ruined walls of a long-derelict building. According to the sector map that Scully carried, it was the remains of slave quarters at a plantation that had once occupied part of the landing area but that had been abandoned many years before.

Private Joe McGurk sat with his back up against moldering brick, scratching his flaming red hair momentarily freed from the confines of the helmet that he clutched between his knees. Visible on the helmet's front were the words Tokyo Or Bust, which he had painted on before the invasion.

McGurk had heard that wearing the helmets all the time made a guy go bald as a cue ball before too long. In fact, McGurk had been noticing clumps of hair falling out at a rapidly increasing rate. Taking a comb from his pocket, he ran it through his hair and inspected the bristles carefully. Strands of curly red hair clung to the plastic bristles of the comb, a reminder to McGurk that even if war didn't kill you, it could still kill a guy's looks.

Lounging a few feet away from McGurk, a private named Finelli slapped at his cheek and cursed the omnipresent mosquitos. Finelli was an Italian from Inglewood, one of the suburbs of Los Angeles. His father had died when he was young, and Finelli had been the sole supporter of his mother and his sister.

At first his mother had not wanted her only son to go to the front and asked him to plead hardship. But Finelli had volunteered for service just the same. His thinking was that if the Japanese could bomb Pearl Harbor, then they could also bomb his mother's house. He couldn't just stand around waiting for the hammer to drop. He had to do something. His mother had cried her eyes out when Finelli boarded the train to boot camp, and she made her son promise to write every day. He did, at least at first.

"Look at the size of this one!" Finelli shouted suddenly, inspecting the squashed insect on his palm. "It's almost as big as a blue jay."

"That's nothing, chimed in Eightball. He had acquired his name not so much because he had been a part-time pool hustler in civilian life but because he often ended up behind the proverbial eight ball in combat situations. Well aware that his name was also military slang for blunders in combat, Eightball accepted his name like a proud badge of defiance, as though it were a king-size chip on his shoulder. "They got tarantulas on these islands that crawl into a guy's sleeping bag at night. They get inside you and start eating your guts from the inside out."

"Shut up, Eightball," McGurk hollered, putting his helmet back on and momentarily forgetting about his hair loss. "I got enough problems worrying about the Japs without worrying about tarantulas, too."

Finelli slapped at his face again and cursed the island's man-eating mosquitoes. "Son of a bitch!" he shouted. "That one was even bigger than the last one!"

The only man in the unit not worrying about the insects was Private First Class Jake Barrows.

The unit's squad gunner, Barrows was responsible for the .30-caliber Browning machine gun that served as the platoon's primary automatic weapon, and he busied himself with the task of oiling and cleaning the Browning while his partner, Mike Papajohn, fitted fresh rounds into an ammo belt.

The Pacific theater of war was the one zone of operations where the Browning MG had been belatedly adopted for use by U.S. regular infantry troops. Until then, it was mostly special units who possessed automatic-fire capability at the squad level other than that provided by the Browning Automatic Rifles carried by regular infantry platoon riflemen.

Before long, Sergeant Scully's hectoring voice was heard among the men bivouacked in the ruins. Scully was telling everybody that it was time to move out.

UP IN THE machine-gun emplacements constructed of heavy logs, the Japanese waited with the patience of stones and the deadliness of tigers. The infantrymen of the Imperial Japanese Army wore steel helmets, with khaki field jackets and high-topped campaign boots completing their combat dress.

Along with his rifle, each officer and NCO carried the *Shin Gunto,* or samurai sword, which, in addition to being used as an offensive weapon, would be put into service to take the soldier's own life if he were in danger of suffering defeat or capture.

General Yamashita, supreme commander of the Japanese forces who had attacked, then occupied, the principal islands of the Philippines chain, had instructed his officers to follow a single rule unfailingly.

The rule was simple: no soldier of Imperial Japan was to be taken alive.

To be captured was to lose face, and that meant the ultimate humiliation that could be inflicted upon a man. For a Japanese soldier to lose face was to suffer a fate far worse than death. Therefore, a soldier in the emperor's army would never surrender.

Death was glorious—indeed, it was a state to which the fighting man should aspire. Captivity, on the other hand, brought a warrior to the depths of ignominy. To the Japanese it represented what was tantamount to a living death.

Captain Hiro Tanaka, commander of forces in the area, had taken the commandment of General Yamashita even a step further. Tanaka had instructed the loyal warriors who served under him to take no less than five of the hated round-eyed enemy with them into the black eternity of death.

As Tanaka hunkered behind a timer barricade that marked the entrance to a forward position facing in the direction of the sea, he studied the movements of the approaching enemy troops through powerful field glasses.

He would withhold the order to open fire on the Americans until they were completely in range of his guns, he decided. Like the tiger in the mountains, he would wait for the unsuspecting prey to come directly toward his lair. Only then would he unsheathe his claws and slaughter them all.

KEEPING HIS TROOPS spread out evenly, Scully penetrated deeper into the steaming jungle depths. The canopy of palms had become interlaced with other tropical trees, and the light was as dim as the humidity was high.

Parrots and other noisy, gaudily plumaged birds flitted from treetop to treetop. The GIs could hear the constant hooting and screeching of the birds and the jabbering of monkeys scurrying around in the treetops overhead, while giant bullfrogs croaked from the swamps beyond the forest. The feeling of steadily mounting tension filled the air like a buildup of static electricity before a thunderstorm.

And then, without warning, the Japanese opened up. Suddenly the air was filled with the chattering death knell of automatic-weapons fire and the surprised grunts and agonized cries of the downed American GIs hit by scything steel. Captain Tanaka, like the tiger of the mountain, had at last bared his deadly claws.

3

Quickly setting up the Browning, Barrows opened fire on the machine-gun emplacement. Now he could clearly see that the bunker was manned by a Japanese weapons detail. In addition to the machine-gun crew, there were soldiers wielding rifles with wickedly honed bayonets fixed to the barrels. But Barrows was certain that he and his .30 caliber could handle the job.

The Browning rattled off a stream of hellfire from its muzzle. The heavy-caliber autoburst caught a Japanese huddling behind sandbag fortifications across the chest, creating a jagged line of spurting red punctures.

"Come and get it!" Barrows roared, elated at having sent the enemy to join his honorable ancestors. His partner, Private Mike Papajohn, fed him more of the belt of ammo, paying it out from the steel ammunition box sitting on the ground at his feet. Barrows continued squeezing off the bursts, pumping a continuous stream of whirling metal studs into the heavily fortified emplacement.

The Japanese were showing full force around the bunker. They were fired up, and their weapons didn't stop belching fire and spitting steel.

From behind a giant coconut palm, an enemy soldier suddenly jumped out at Eightball. His lean, triangular face was contorted in a fearsome snarl, and his eyes glittered like polished jet. He was a big man, not like the slight Japanese usually depicted in Hollywood movies.

With a ferocious yell, he charged at Eightball banzai-style. The bayonet sticking out from the end of the rifle was long, sharp and aimed straight for Eightball's throat. It had runnels on the flats that would run with hot blood when the bayonet struck home. The enemy knew how to use the lethal weapon, and Eightball could tell that he meant business.

Angling his body, Eightball sidestepped in a single fluid motion of upper body and legs just the way they had drilled him in boot camp. On the follow-through, he brought up the heavy wooden buttstock of his Garand rifle and used the power in his hands and muscular arms to bring the buttstock crashing hard against his opponent's jaw.

"Aieeee!" the man screamed as his jaw shattered with an ugly whunking sound. But he hadn't been put out of commission yet. Bleeding profusely from a serious head wound but still conscious, he tried to whip his service revolver from the holster at his belt.

But Eightball was quicker on the draw. Sliding the long dagger from the canvas sheath on his thigh, he stooped and plunged the dagger straight into the soldier's throat. For a moment the man shivered all over, and again Eightball brought the dagger down and plunged it through the abdomen. He only stopped when his opponent ceased moving and lay dead on the ground.

Scully and Mockler found themselves face-to-face with a group of Japanese who had emerged unexpectedly out of the underbrush. Their strategy was to surround and overwhelm the Americans.

The enemy soldiers had been squatting in their foxholes, their faces smeared with mud, their helmets camouflaged with snippets of brush and fern sticking out from the netting on their helmets. Patiently and silently they had waited for the Americans to walk headlong into the trap they had prepared.

Reacting almost instantly, Scully turned and discharged the tommy gun point-blank into a soldier who was running at him swinging a samurai sword and yelling louder than Scully had heard any man ever yell. The autoburst of .45-caliber rippers from the Thompson SMG hit the swordsman squarely in the stomach, stopping the bloodcurdling war cries as his insides were torn apart.

As he fell aside and hit the dirt on his face, another Japanese dropped down into a one-handed shooting stance and began blasting Scully with his rifle.

With bullets buzzing and whining around him like a swarm of angry steel hornets, Scully zigged and zagged about, then took a flying jump that landed his rump in a ditch concealed by a wall of man-high island grass.

Reaching for one of the grenades hanging on his chest webbing, he bit the ring of the cotter pin between his side teeth and pulled hard, then lobbed the waffled steel pineapple with a sidearm pitch.

The grenade sailed across space, landed a few feet from the Japanese soldier, then bounced three times. The deadly pineapple went off four seconds later with a solid crump, and Scully saw the shooter hurled into the air and fall back into the grass again seconds later with a sickening thud.

Already up from cover and running, Scully rotored more slugs at the charging enemy, who were firing their rifles and swinging their swords with frightening speed.

But it was hot lead instead of cold steel that decided the issue as Scully's tommy burst took out two of them immediately. Throwing up their arms, they did a crazy, jerky dance like drunken Kabuki dancers before their legs folded beneath them as they toppled lifelessly into the high parched grass.

Two were down but the third one was still too much alive for Scully's good. The Japanese soldier was throwing fire from the small automatic pistol clutched in his fist. The man had lost his helmet, and his closely shaven skull, gaunt cheeks and burning black eyes made him look like the very incarnation of the angel of death.

Aiming the tommy gun at the specter, Scully pumped the SMG's trigger, but to no avail. Like some cantankerous mule who balks in the middle of a steep climb, Scully's weapon had chosen that instant to run dry.

Cursing a blue streak, he wasted no time in ducking down below the line of fire. But Scully's moment of hesitation had given the enemy the chance to score a hit. Even as Scully made like the wind and blew, a slug caught him on the shoulder, high up in the flesh and muscle just below the collarbone. Blood spurted through the torn shreds of his khaki fatigues in a sick, hot stream. Wounded now and with no time to reload, Scully threw down the tommy gun and switched to backup armament.

Hunkering behind some fallen rocks, Scully pulled his GI-issue Colt M1911A1 automatic pistol from his chest holster. There was no need to retract then release the Colt's slide because he always kept a round chambered. Maybe it was a dangerous practice, but with a powerful automatic like the Colt .45, Scully always figured it was far more dangerous to pause the extra few seconds it took to work the slide action and crank one into the pipe.

In a single fluid motion the sergeant thumbed back the Colt's hammer and held the large-frame automatic pistol at the ready.

He didn't have to wait long for his chance at the brass ring to come around. The Japanese soldier was stalking him, duck-walking through the high grass with his autopistol poised for instant deployment, sweeping left and right at his belt line in a dangerous arc.

The man's glittering eyes were alert to every movement in the grass, primed to detect any telltale sign of the presence of the American GI whom he knew to be hiding in the *kunai* stands somewhere just ahead of him. His whole body was in a state of high alarm, primed for reflex action. The barrel of his pistol waved back and forth, ready to instantly target the enemy and blow him right off the face of the earth.

Then, when the man's eyes had swept past his hiding place, Scully jumped up and pumped the trigger of the Colt, emptying its clip of .45s into his opponent's torso. The effect of this barrage was to riddle the enemy with holes and end the contest then and there. The mortally wounded man collapsed to the ground in the last throes of death.

The rest of the men dealt with their own attackers, relying on speed, determination and presence of mind. In a short while only the enemy machine-gun position was left as the major obstacle in the platoon's advance.

4

Barrows's Browning machine gun was maintaining a constant chatter, but the Japanese were still holed up in the bunker and showed no sign of being dislodged. The net result was that Third Platoon was pinned down and impeded on their front flank, and that made them sitting ducks in a big way.

Artillery from gun batteries positioned farther inland was beginning to drop shells near them, too. At first the shelling was haphazard and desultory, but then the high-explosive shells began coming closer and closer together and with increasingly greater accuracy as the gun batteries got their quarry taped.

So far, the enemy had been holding back because of the proximity of the fighting to their own line formations. But their forward artillery spotters must have alerted them to the fact that their forces were being wiped out and that the survivors had already fled into the jungle.

"To hell with this chickenshit stuff," Barrows shouted, frustrated and angered by the stalemate. "Papajohn, how many rounds we got left?"

Papajohn checked the contents of the ammo box. "Couple of hundred, chief." Papajohn watched Barrows strip off his pack, followed by his field jacket, after which he threw down his sweat-stained and mud-spattered khaki shirt.

"Say, what's the idea?" Papajohn inquired when Barrows was naked above the waist.

"I once won a medal running the fifty-yard dash on my high school track team," Barrows said. "I'm going to try and see if I can beat my old record. Give my regards to Broadway."

Working quickly once he had stripped off his gear, Barrows pulled the heavy Browning off the ground and hefted it, feeling the heat of the barrel quickly penetrate the canvas gloves he wore to protect his hands. The barrel was burning hot, but he didn't judge the weapon to be in any danger of cooking off the ammo supply.

"Guess you want me to cover you, chief," Papajohn said.

"I sure don't want you to blow me kisses," Barrows answered, his eyes on the terrain ahead.

With the Browning now cradled in his arms, he jumped up and started running toward the gun emplacement at full gallop. His features were contorted, showing determination and wild exhilaration. A terrifying war cry emanated from his throat. Bloodcurdling, it was part rebel yell and part lunatic banshee scream, a cry that came from somewhere deep and primitive in his warrior's soul.

"See you in hell, you dirty Japs!" he shouted as he raced headlong at the enemy emplacement set in the side of the hill. The stream of heavy-caliber rounds was now pouring from his Browning, the barrel belched smoke and fire in addition to lethal steel.

The Japanese were firing back at the charging American, determined to stop him in his tracks. The entire crew of the heavily fortified machine-gun emplacement was bent on pouring automatic fire on the single GI who was advancing on them.

Scully followed Barrows's progress from cover, shaking his head at the foolhardy bravery. Privates McGurk and Pee Wee Drummond and Corporal Mockler watched with transfixed expressions. Their faces mirrored what every man among them believed: Barrows had gone out of his cotton-picking mind.

"Okay, boys, cover Barrows!" Scully shouted a second later. He had already loaded a fresh drum magazine of .45-caliber rounds into the receiver of the Thompson SMG and had cocked the first round into the chamber. A trigger-pull set it chattering, and a lethal hail of lead and fire belched forth, unerringly aimed at the enemy.

The rattle of Scully's automatic weapon was soon joined by the full fury of massed fire from BARs, Garands and Thompsons ported by the surviving members of the platoon. Backed by full cover fire, Barrows continued his suicide run toward the firebase surrounded by a hail of whirlwinding steel thrown by his buddies from the rear and cheered on by a wild chorus of shouts and whistles.

Barrows was almost on top of the machine-gun nest. Big as life, he saw the troops behind the sandbags aiming the big Taisho-3 machine gun. The Taisho-3 was also called the "Woodpecker" because of its distinctively slow and steady rate of fire. The heavy-caliber machine gun was mounted on a tripod, its legs buried deep in the soft, yielding sand. But the enemy fire didn't strike him. Against all odds, Barrows was getting through.

The Browning SMG in his hands was taking a deadly toll on the enemy's troops. One of the defenders climbed behind the machine gun and began pouring on the hot steel rivets, but suddenly clutched his chest and toppled sideways as .30-caliber steeljackets riddled him through and through.

Another soldier pushed him aside to take his place, but he was also cut down by the Browning's stream of deadly fire immediately. One by one, the Taisho-3 acquired new gunners to unleash its blazing fire, and one by one the gunners were taken out, tossed aside by the fury of hot slugs.

"I believe Barrows is going to make it after all, Sarge," Corporal Mockler said as he reloaded his Garand rifle, shouting to be heard above the terrible din of the firefight raging around them.

"Keep shooting!" Scully shouted at his troops. "He's almost close enough to kick them right in the balls."

The platoon, dodging enemy fire behind their makeshift barricades, could see Barrows reach the site of the enemy bunker. The burning-hot muzzle of the chattering Browning in his fists was almost com-

pletely level with the fire-breathing muzzle of the
Japanese machine gun raised off the ground on its
tripod mount.

Bringing around the muzzle of the Browning, Barrows launched a salvo of hot .30-caliber lead straight
into the dark depths of the bunker. The gunner behind the machine gun took a hit in the head, and before another could take his place, Barrows pulled out
a grenade and lobbed it into the bunker. As the grenade sailed into its yawning depths, Barrows dodged
to one side. The fragmentation bomb's explosion sent
chips of shattered timber and fractured stone blowing
from the mouth of the bunker.

"Up and at 'em!" Scully bellowed like an angry bull
as he leapt up from concealment, firing his tommy.
"Show them what you're made of!"

With a savage war whoop from every man, the rest
of Scully's platoon came charging hell-bent for leather
up the slope of the high ground. When they reached
the bunker, they saw that the gun emplacement had
been erected at the mouth of a natural limestone cavern. Inside the cavern were meandering side caverns,
explaining how the gunners manning the machine gun
were able to take turns behind the trigger in an unbro-
ken stream.

But enemy soldiers were still holed up inside the
cavern. One of them emerged out of the dimness suddenly and came running on a suicide strike. Stripped
to the waist, he wore what they called a "Scarf of a
Thousand Stitches" around his waist—a hand-painted

silk sheet made by their womenfolk as battle talismans.

As he charged the GIs, he shouted and brandished two potato-masher-style grenades in his hands. The GIs scattered, discharging their guns, as the enemy lunged at them, but he managed to grab Private Arty Basset around the shoulders, his lean though sinewy arms grasping the private in a grip as strong as iron with the grenades jammed into the small of his back.

Basset squirmed and twisted, but he was locked in his opponent's grip as surely as if iron chains bound him. They fell rolling and thrashing onto the rough stone floor of the cavern. A moment later there was an explosion in which Basset and his adversary were blown to pieces.

"Don't look at Basset!" Scully shouted at his soldiers. "You know who did it to him. Take it out on the Japs! Make them pay for every drop of blood!"

Other Japanese were not so kamikaze-minded as the soldier who had turned himself into a human suicide bomb. Intent on saving a desperate situation, they blasted their guns at the enemy. But their actions were prompted more by panic than serious defensive strategy, and they were blown to ragged bloody pieces by the hailstorm of American lead directed against them in lethal answer. The cavern became a grim burial crypt, with the dead strewn like cordwood all over the naked rock floor.

Scully looked around him once the shooting had finally stopped. The cavern complex was truly gigantic, as large as anything man-made—maybe even as big as the Malinta tunnel complex on Corregidor— and perfectly suited for a military command center. Scully ordered Mockler to form a detail and scout for maps or any other Intelligence that could be useful to their side. After everything salvageable had been confiscated from the enemy, they would blow the place to destroy anything that could be used by the enemy in the future.

One thing they didn't have to worry about was dealing with prisoners of war. The Japanese soldier didn't believe in letting himself be taken alive. The cave complex was littered with the bodies of the enemy who had committed suicide. The GI Joes of the Sunshine Division prepared to bid the enemy a blazing *sayonara*.

5

The sun was already high in the sky, burning with intensity as the platoon advanced from the recently secured cave complex.

Third Platoon had lost a couple of men so far. But casualties were the universal coinage of war, and the men had been prepared to pay their dues. Considering how determinedly and how savagely the enemy had resisted the American assault, the men of Blackjack Company's Third Platoon had acquitted themselves extremely well and had succeeded in keeping casualty levels within reasonable limits.

According to Scully's sector map, the Japanese command post that was the platoon's secondary objective lay approximately a half mile to the south. The CP housed ammunition for a troop garrison and a radio station. The radio station could be used to call in Zero fighter aircraft and artillery fire from island batteries, as well.

Scully put the map back into his pocket and shouted for the men of his platoon to fall in behind. They had been taking a brief rest period, but it was time to move on again, to walk that next mile to the next dying place—the foot soldier's lot in the bloody labor of war.

They marched through dense jungle, relying on their knives to hack their way through choking vegetation. In a short while the platoon came within shouting distance of the Japanese troop garrison.

The layout of the troop garrison followed the general design of such installations on the Pacific islands controlled by the Imperial Japanese Army.

It consisted of a complex of round huts with peaked roofs made out of palm thatching. Most of the thatched roofs were still green in coloration, indicating that the huts had been recently erected. In front of the largest of these structures, hoisted to the top of a white-painted bamboo mast, flew the colors of Imperial Japan—the red orb of the rising sun against a background of white.

Several barracks longhouses with raised porches housed the soldiers. The longhouses were built on stilts to limit exposure to seasonal flooding. The installation's ratio center was in a tin-roofed shack with a long steel antenna pylon about twenty-five feet high standing beside it. The pylon was linked by cables to the radio shack.

Neither Scully nor the other GIs saw any sign of life. But they were well aware that they had been observed. Most likely the Japanese were using the cover of natural terrain features to advance unseen and surround the enemy before commencing an attack.

It was a style of fighting that was considerably unlike most combat encounters in the European theater. Guerrilla fighting there was primarily a tactic used by irregular forces and partisan groups. American line soldiers at the platoon level rarely had to contend with an enemy who fought in this particular fashion.

It went against the American grain, which was more naturally geared to up-front confrontations than to those based on stealth and concealment. An entirely new psychology of combat would have to be developed to fight the enemy in this new way.

But the men of Blackjack Company, like Americans fighting everywhere in the Pacific, were fast learners. Any tactic that was used against them, they instantly imitated, then improved on, and finally turned it against the enemy with an extra twist or two of their own thrown in for good measure.

Tension filled the air as the GIs started cautiously wading through a shallow bog overgrown with high grass and surrounded by a tall canebrake on all sides. Suddenly the sloshing sounds of water were drowned out by a barrage of small-arms fire. Swearing, the men hefted their weapons to return fire.

Japanese infantrymen began appearing everywhere through the waving curtain of sugarcane. The dirt paths running between the high rows of sugarcane resounded with the battle cries of men fighting hand-to-hand over a patch of contested ground. Rifle butts were utilized in crushing blows, and bayonets found their targets in the vulnerable, unprotected bodies. Blood flowed freely, glistening brightly in the sun.

Two American GIs, Tweedy and Yunker, found themselves on the fringes of the fight. They were confronted by three Japanese soldiers who appeared ready to surrender.

"Shoot them!" Tweedy advised his buddy Yunker, brandishing his rifle. "Get them before they shoot us!"

"Naw, they want to surrender, Tweedy. See, their hands are up in the air."

Tweedy moved forward and was about to frisk the enemy troops when the Japanese soldier in the center of the group suddenly bent down. In a split second the two GIs realized that a black machine pistol was tied behind the crouching man's back. Before they could act, the Japanese on the left reached over and grabbed the concealed weapon. A trigger pull, and the two GIs were stitched with steel and fell to the ground in thrashing, bleeding heaps.

Immediately the three Japanese pulled long daggers and fell on the badly wounded GIs. The enemy's daggers extinguished any signs of life in the Americans. Their bloody work completed, they moved off into the waving ranks of sugarcane and disappeared like shadows.

The main body of the U.S. landing force had already breached the bamboo perimeter fence of the base and penetrated into the graveled compound that formed an apron around the large cylindrical hut that served as the installation's headquarters. Japanese soldiers were massed there, ready to make it a fight to the finish. Several officers were shouting orders to the ranks in quick succession. The men responded with a wild cheer and waved their weapons in the air.

But determination alone was not sufficient to win the battle. Massed American fire and rifle grenades started cutting down the enemy, and they formed bloodied heaps on the ground. The command post, though badly damaged by fire, still remained standing, and inside the radio shack the Japanese operator was frantically relaying an SOS message.

He was on the line to an airbase located farther inland. The airbase was also under heavy attack, but its squadron of Zeros had managed to get airborne before the attack had come. At that moment they were streaking through the skies toward the besieged installation. There was still time to make the enemy pay dearly for his victory no matter what the cost in flesh and blood.

6

McGurk and Applebaum kicked in the flimsy door of the radio shack. Even as they cautiously entered the gloomy interior, a trooper with an autorifle was hurling lead at them. Applebaum dodged the whining bullets and answered the burst by pulling the trigger of his own M-1.

He got lucky on his first try. The M-1 salvo punched the trooper right through the midsection, and he dropped his weapon as he staggered backward, then collapsed to the floor.

The radio operator quickly turned from his frantic SOS delivery and grabbed a loaded pistol lying within reach on the table in front of him. He raised the weapon and aimed it at the two khaki-clad intruders, but he never had the opportunity to pull the trigger. McGurk's shot tumbled him onto the table with his arms spread out, slack and useless.

"The sarge says we have to demolish this place," McGurk said to Applebaum after making sure that no more surprises lay in store.

"Check," Applebaum returned. He was already getting down to business, reloading his weapon and cranking round number one into the M-1's firing chamber.

McGurk followed suit and snapped a reload into his own weapon, and they leveled their weapons and riddled the radio equipment with volleys of .30-caliber steel. Bullets punched through the olive drab housings of the commo gear, and acrid smoke, shot through with hot blue sparks, soon began billowing from the perforated radio units.

When their rifles had run out of bullets, McGurk and Applebaum pulled two Mk-IIA1 fragmentation grenades apiece from shoulder webbing. They yanked the pins out with their teeth, then spit out the pins.

They raised the deadly submunitions, hearing the tinny *thik-thik-thik* sounds of the spoons disengaging from the pin assembly, and lobbed the pineapples underhand into the radio shack and dived for cover to either side of the structure.

The grenades bounced and rolled across the floor, and then suddenly they exploded with a single, terrific bang that blew the glass windows of the radio shack out of their frames and echoed like a thunderclap through the jungle clearing. The radio mast was still left standing, and Applebaum and McGurk attached grenades to its base, making up cluster charges of three grenades each and taping the charges to the legs supporting the mast.

A tug on one of the cotter pins, and McGurk ran like hell to join Applebaum behind the cover of a rusting bulldozer. Just as McGurk hit the dirt, the grenades went off with a loud kuhh-*blam,* and the ra-

dio mast toppled to the ground with the groan of ruptured, twisting metal and a final earsplitting crash.

All over the compound of the captured base, U.S.
troops were engaged in the job of mopping up the remaining resistance. As had previously been the case,
none of the Japanese surrendered, except for those
who had been wounded in action.

The only sign of the enemy in the compound was
casualties and dead men. The rest of the defenders had
disappeared into the fields of high grass and native
cane that stood on the periphery of the thatch-roofed
bamboo command post main building. Corporal
Mockler was busy with the mop-up operations when
he looked up at the sky. He'd heard the telltale droning of the Zeros' powerful Mitsubishi engines before
and knew what it heralded.

He shouted at the rest of the unit to dodge for cover.
He realized that the enemy planes would be upon them
in a matter of seconds. A heartbeat later, as the GIs
went flying for cover, the Zeros were on them like a
swarm of angry wasps, guns blazing and chattering
out a grim song of vengeance.

Crouching beside a high coconut palm that rose at
the edge of a stand of cane, Private Tommy Wyszynski looked up and fired at an oncoming Zero. The
Browning Automatic Rifle jumped in his hands, and
he saw the incandescent tracer rounds that were loaded
at the top of the clip stray up into the sky and a couple of the rounds strike the Zero's wings.

But the Zero kept on coming straight for him, swooping down so low that its boiler-plate underbody almost skirted the waving tops of the shoulder-high sugarcane.

The next moment the Zero was almost on top of Wyszynski. The Japanese attack fighter was so close that Wyszynski could make out the outline of the pilot's face behind the glass bubble of the cockpit. He thought he could see the sneer of contempt and fierce hatred that contorted the face of the enemy.

Wyszynski considered running, but time seemed to stand still. He seemed frozen in place, unable to move. It was as though his feet were held fast to the muddy earth on which he stood like the roots of the sugarcane plants around him. Suddenly flame belched from the machine-gun ports located at the front of the Japanese attack plane, and the GI's moment of truth came in a terrible burst of heat and light and sound.

A heavy weight, an invisible weight wielded by a giant he could not see, struck him in the center of his chest. With a groan of pain he was catapulted backward into the field of rustling sugarcane as the Zero roared over his head, belching contrails of smoke from its engine cowling.

Wyszynski half turned on his side and looked up. He had lost his BAR as the bullets had thudded into him. He put his hands out in an unconscious gesture of protection. His lips were forming the words, *Don't, don't!* but no sound issued from them. He saw the

Zero swing around and come at him for a second strafing run.

The first bullets struck the ground a few yards away. They thudded toward Wyszynski with the precise alignment of beads on a string—beads of sudden death. Japanese lead hit the writhing figure on the ground and continued on, leaving Wyszynski a still, lifeless thing. The Zero gained altitude, circled and came swooping back down again to hunt for fresh prey.

Closer to the secured compound, Scully was standing with legs splayed, his tommy gun held in a classic rifleman's stance with the buttstock jammed against his shoulder blade. He squinted along the sights to aim at yet another Zero attack plane heading toward him.

Twin lines of ground-thwacking bullets kicked up clods of mud and splinters of pulverized, spinning rock as the pilot triggered his forward guns at the American below him. Scully stood firm and continued to hold his fire.

"Come a little closer!" he shouted between clenched teeth. "Just a little fucking closer." The Zeros were notoriously underarmored, and at close range even standard rife ammunition could inflict significant damage, while a .50-caliber burst could cause the fighter planes to disintegrate.

Then the Zero was dead on him, and Scully opened up with the chattering tommy gun clutched in his white-knuckled hands. His first short burst of .45-caliber whizzers stitched across the Plexiglas canopy cockpit bubble of the Zero, splintering it to a mass of fractures. Scully saw sudden red shower against the shattered windshield of the cockpit as the pilot sagged to one side.

Yelling and screaming, Scully continued to pour a stream of fire into the Zero as it suddenly veered wildly, went down skidding on its belly and crashed into a giant coconut palm tree some distance away.

The cockpit of the crashed plane opened up, and the pilot, whose face was a mask of dark, shining blood, climbed out shakily. As he saw Scully approach, he pulled a pistol from a canvas chest rig strapped across his flight suit and raised it toward the American with surprising speed.

Scully had the tommy gun in position and was ready to let the pilot have it when the flyboy suddenly raised the pistol to his own head and pulled the trigger with a smile of triumph on his face. Instantly his head shattered with a spray of blood, and he sagged against the fuselage of the crashed plane and slid down onto the ground.

But facing off with the enemy's air power wasn't the sole measure taken by the platoon. Sparks was on the unit's radio to the aircraft carriers anchored offshore. The message was received, and a squadron of P-47s was being dispatched to counter the attack. There were too many of the enemy's planes and not enough of the GIs, who were not properly equipped to combat them, geared instead to the securing of a ground-based objective.

The squadron of P-47s was on its way, lifting off from the decks. Now all the platoon had to do was survive until they got there. But surviving against the determined Japanese was the hardest task they had to face. The platoon had its work cut out.

7

"Okay, boys," Matt Heacocks, the squadron leader, said into his microphone, "I've got visual contact with the Zeros. Let's close in."

"Roger on that," the wingman of the squadron of P-47s answered. Moments later the squadron veered down from the clouds and closed fast on the enemy.

On the ground the GIs sent up a clamorous cheer as they saw the American P-47s closing in on the attacking Zeros. But the strafing continued as the Japanese seemed intent on attacking the men on the ground despite the sudden presence of the fast and deadly American fighter aircraft.

But danger didn't only come from the skies. Many of the Japanese soldiers who had drifted into the jungle and canebrakes surrounding the garrison's perimeter during the attack on the compound were returning with reinforcements from stations deeper in the jungle. Renewed ground fighting had broken out, hot and fast and deadly.

Scully's platoon, harried both from the ground and from the air, severely depleted in ammunition reserves from the fighting so far, was pressing on at a great disadvantage. But they had no choice—caught between a two-pronged attack, there was no stopping now except to die. While the aerial dogfight raged in the skies overhead, the men of Blackjack Company's Third Platoon had their hands full dealing with Japanese troopers stalking them from the jungle's edge.

It seemed as though they were closing in from every direction at the same time. The giant fronds of enormous tropical plants parted, and then the emperor's soldiers dashed out, brandishing rifles, swords and bayonet knives, thirsting for American blood and eager to wreak revenge for being driven off.

The menace of the savage war cries issuing from their throats as they closed in on the encircled GI forces was underscored by the long bayonets affixed to their rifles.

"Judas Priest and Christmas crackers, Sarge," Private Jim Anson cried out as he looked north, south, east and west to see the enemy popping up everywhere. "The Nips got this place surrounded!"

"I can see that for myself, doughfoot," Scully growled back. "Now quit readin' me the news and let's get some of these schmoes from Tokyo."

Saying that, Scully cut loose with a long, chattering burst of tommy-gun fire at two infantrymen who were running at him, cold steel in their hands and battle cries on their lips. As they charged, plainly meaning to skewer him through the chest with their fixed bayonets, they also discharged their bolt-action rifles.

Suddenly a bullet burned against Scully's stomach, leaving a raw red groove that smarted with the stinging sensation of fire. It was the second time he'd been wounded since landing on the island, and Scully was hopping mad. Twin fires burned him now. The first from his fresh wound, the second from somewhere deep within his raging warrior's heart.

A burst of his tommy gun found a target in the attacker who'd fired his rifle and sent hot lead lancing through him. His partner now saw the better part of valor and suddenly ducked behind the cover of a shattered building wall and resumed firing his rifle from a protected crouch.

But Scully had already pulled a hand grenade, and he pitched the pineapple over the top of the shattered wall. The grenade went off with a burst of lethal shrapnel, and the firing stopped abruptly.

Anson was knocked to the ground as he tripped over a large tree root when he dodged the swing of a bayonet. As the enemy pointed the business end of his rifle downward to fire, Anson drew his service pistol from belt leather and, in a blast of white heat, made the rifleman's face disintegrate into a red mist. Springing to his feet, the GI hardly had time to get his bearings when he was stabbed right through the kidneys.

The Japanese soldier pulled out his long bayonet and let Anson have it again with a bullet through the stomach. Cursing and groaning, he toppled to the ground, and the attacker prepared for the final shot. Managing to summon his last reserves of remaining strength, Anson lashed out with his leg and slammed his boot squarely into his executioner's unguarded groin. The man let out a high-pitched howl, lost his footing and tumbled across his victim.

Anson reached up and grabbed him with the vise-like grip of the dying. His steely fingers held the squirming man as tightly as bands of iron as he groped for chest webbing and closed his forefinger around the cotter pin ring of an Mk-IIA1 fragmentation grenade.

"You dirty Nip bastard! I'll see you in hell!" he rasped, seeing wild fear pool in the widened eyes of the Japanese soldier. A moment later an explosion blew both struggling antagonists from white-hot hell straight into cold black eternity.

At the other end of the battlefield, Barrows and Papajohn had set up the Browning .30 and were swinging the chattering automatic weapon around in a deadly steel-hiccuping arc.

The enfilading fire that was cranked out by the heavy gun cut down the Japanese left and right as they charged the gun emplacement. Snarling and yelling as they charged, the suicidal soldiers continued to come on as fast as Barrows could cut them down to size with the .30-caliber hellfire he threw at them nonstop.

Near the field of sugarcane that flanked the captured Japanese command post on one side, many members of Third Platoon, including Jacek and Pee Wee Drummond, had their hands full dealing with the charging foot soldiers and strafing Zeros alike.

Jacek's life was on the line when he suddenly ran out of rifle bullets. One of the enemy took advantage of the situation and pulled a Kiska-type grenade and prepared to hurl it.

Before he could follow through, a Zero chose that instant to come sweeping down on a strafing run. As the Americans ran for cover, a stray bullet caught the Japanese who was holding the grenade, readied for a straight-armed pitch. Laid open by shrapnel from throat to groin by friendly fire, he was unable to pitch the grenade. It cooked off, catching his comrades in the killing blast. The steep-diving Zero pulled out of its downward plunge, and immediately a P-47 gave chase.

The Japanese pilot was good, which wasn't always the case because the Japanese were forced to strap green recruits into the cockpits. Seeing that the American plane was hot on his tail, he put the Zero through a series of jinks and loops and succeeded in evading the U.S. fighter aircraft. But not for long. The contest had already been decided with the superior armament and maneuverability of the P-47 and the superior piloting ability of the American sky jockey.

The P-47 stuck to the Zero's tail like a shadow at high noon and finally wound up the chase with a burst from its front-mounted machine guns that chewed up most of the Zero's tail section and riddled its fuselage.

Dense black smoke began to pour from the Zero's engine cowling as the pilot bailed out. The Sunshine Division troops looked up and saw the fighter crash through stands of coconut palm and send up a churning plume of orange-black fire. Smoke and flames rose from among the forest trees in the aftermath of the crash-and-burn, and a contrail of black smoke drifted overhead, high in the blue tropical sky.

The pilot of the downed Zero was another matter. His chute had opened without a hitch, and the pilot had sailed lazily down to earth. Scully's men saw that he would come down in the middle of a nearby cane-brake.

Determined to make a capture, members of Third Platoon plunged into the waving sugarcane stalks to hunt down their prey. They caught up with the pilot finally after a long chase. He bowed to them, then straightened up with a pistol in his hand.

Already wise to such tactics, Pee Wee let him have it with a bullet that opened up a third, blood-red eye in the center of his head. Flinging his arms straight out as though he were preparing to take wing, the pilot flopped down to the ground and lay still.

The dogfight had wound to a close, every enemy plane having been taken out of commission. Barrows and Papajohn finally saw the few infantrymen left alive beginning to retreat into the jungle. The rest of the Japanese dead lay piled up all around the machine-gun emplacement. Only now could the platoon's objective be said to be finally secured.

8

Lieutenant Mack Bloodworth looked up and watched as a detail trundled down the colors of the Imperial Japanese Empire and hoisted the red, white and blue in its place. He saluted Old Glory. He had already given orders for burial details to be formed and a field hospital set up to tend to the wounded.

As was their usual custom, the Japanese had not surrendered, preferring a glorious death in battle to capture and imprisonment. Among the wounded of this engagement, there were no Japanese troops at all. Bloodworth's own men had suffered heavy casualties in taking and securing the installation. The enemy was brave—no doubt about that.

But they were certainly also somewhat insane by Western standards of behavior. Furthermore, it wasn't sound leadership to waste troops in suicidal and therefore pointless attacks on the enemy's position. That was one among many reasons why Bloodworth had no doubt that the Japanese colors would not be flying over the Pacific for very much longer.

Already the U.S. fighting man had been bloodied in violent combat at places like Guadalcanal, sending the Japanese reeling from the blow. Soon the colors of the rising sun would be coming down from flagpoles everywhere in the region and the red, white and blue hoisted to fly proudly in their place.

Several B-Company men had been killed in action during the fight to take the objective. Many more had been wounded in the battle. The lists of the company's wounded included Sergeant Matt Scully, whom Bloodworth was going to put in for a second Purple Heart due to his bravery under fire.

In his opinion Barrows deserved the Bronze Star for his machine-gun charge of the Japanese bunker early in the engagement. Either that or a section eight.

Bloodworth set out on a tour of the secured enemy position. Once on the scene, he busily issued orders and answered questions from his men. The most persistent of these questions concerned the arrival of reinforcements.

The lieutenant aimed to find out the answer himself as he turned on his heels and walked up the steps that led to the main bamboo hut of the former Japanese command post. It had remained intact enough to serve as a temporary headquarters.

One corner of the structure was now set aside to house the radioman's equipment. Blowing up the enemy's radio transmitter tower had been a rash action, even though the privates responsible had not known better. Fortunately the tower had been largely salvaged by company engineers, and Sparks was able to hook up his own radio equipment to it. With communications available at last, Bloodworth ordered

Sparks to raise the battalion commander, Major Duncan Loudermilk.

"Good work, Mack," Loudermilk told Bloodworth from his position at the north end of the island landing zone. "Congratulate your men for me, too. I know you and your troops were handed a dirty job. If it's any consolation, I also knew that only the best men could handle it."

"Thank you, sir. I'll pass that along to the men," Bloodworth said into the mike, then in a more grave tone of voice, went on, "We need reinforcements badly, sir, as well as medicine, food supplies and ammunition."

"Consider it on its way, Lieutenant. A relief column is being readied even as we speak. The Japs shouldn't be giving you any trouble, at least not for a while. Fresh troops and supplies will be there by tomorrow."

After signing off, Bloodworth left the unit's new headquarters and stepped out into the baking hot sun of late afternoon. He looked around and shook his head, finding it strange that in the aftermath of battle the place seemed almost peaceful now that the casualties had been cleared away. Yet only recently men had bled and died by the dozen while planes wheeled about in the sky.

Beneath the waving palm fronds, flanked by masses of brown-green *kunai* grass beneath the hot tropical sun that shone down out of a clear blue sky, it was almost as if nothing of the violence of war had touched the primeval stillness of the jungle.

But cries that came from the field hospital—cries from the mouths of his troops wounded in the brutal action of the assault—quickly dispelled the illusion. The specter of war had indeed touched this island in the Pacific, Bloodworth realized with a start, just as it had touched the rest of the world with its cruel realities. Before peace came to the Pacific again, more men would give their lives, he knew.

A shadow fell across the lieutenant, and suddenly Bloodworth realized that Scully was standing there, saying something to him. Damned odd how a man's mind wandered in these conditions, he thought as he turned to face the soldier.

"What was that, Sergeant?" he asked Scully.

"I was saying that considering how we're in this jungle paradise and there ain't too many Japs around, how about giving me permission to form a hunting detail. There's probably a lot of game in the jungle, sir."

"Good idea, Scully," Bloodworth admitted. "Except for one thing. Who's going to cook it?"

Scully grinned and pointed to himself, but suddenly winced with pain. His recent wounds were signaling for him to slow down. But he shrugged it off. "Me, sir," he replied without hesitation. "'Wild game à la Scully.' The men won't forget the chow I'll dish up for a long time."

"I'm sure they won't," Bloodworth said heartily. "Get to it, Sergeant."

SCULLY, EIGHTBALL and Finelli set out in search of game. The jungle was close and dark, and there didn't seem to be any sign of animal life as they hacked their way through its dense foliage. And then, just as they were about to call it quits, the three GIs heard a snuffling sound coming from somewhere up ahead and a rustling noise in the jungle underbrush. At first they thought that it was the enemy and instantly put themselves on the alert.

Then with a shock they realized that the commotion had been caused by a pack of wild jungle boars. The boars were nuzzling the ground as they grubbed about for roots and tubers. Stealing up on the hairy piglike creatures, Eightball, Finelli and Scully watched as two boars faced off and, with grunts, squeals and the clatter and clash of their razor-sharp tusks, lowered their heads and charged at each other.

They circled around the herd that was distracted by the struggle and then summarily opened fire on the whole pack. They succeeded in felling three of the big, long-tusked boars with the scattershot hunting technique. The herd took off into the jungle, disappearing without a trace in seconds.

Eightball was anxious to see their prize. He set off at a trot, but he tripped and went crashing to the ground.

"What the hell!" he shouted angrily as he fell on his shoulder, cutting his jaw on the sharp root of a projecting tree trunk. Reaching out to lift himself off the ground, he felt something hard and angular.

His anger suddenly turned to curiosity. Ignoring his injury, he began to dig around in the leaf-littered ground and soon uncovered a concealed cache of earthen jugs.

Pulling one of the the jugs from the hole in the ground, Eightball pulled the cork that sealed its mouth with his teeth and took a whiff. To his surprise and delight the stuff smelled drinkable. He decided to chance a slug and tipped back the jug for a drink. It tasted odd, but he took another slug.

The second slug made his insides burst into flame and his head spin. By the time he'd had a third hit from the bottle, it started tasting downright drinkable. In fact, it was starting to taste pretty damned good.

"What the hell is *that* you got there, Eightball?" Scully asked as he and Finelli gathered around.

"Some kind of Jap jungle hooch," Eightball said with a silly grin, then took another swig from the jug.

"Give that here," Scully demanded. "For all you know this could be some kind of Nip booby trap. Let an expert take a look-see."

Eightball handed the jug over and wiped his mouth with the back of his hand. Scully spit out the first gulp he took. Methodically, with a great show, he took another swallow. He made a sour face, but a couple more swigs later found that he was of the same opinion as Eightball. The jungle hooch left behind by the enemy sure lit a fire in a man.

9

The following day the replacements arrived at last. To assist in garrisoning the newly captured Japanese position, Blackjack Company's Second Platoon had also been marched in to beef up the ranks.

As far as Third Platoon went, its personnel received the much-needed replacements that had been requested by Lieutenant Bloodworth. They quickly learned that two of the replacements were unusual men indeed. Scully found that out for himself when, roused from a catnap in a makeshift hammock he'd slung between two coconut palms, he came over to see what all the commotion was about in the compound that morning. He witnessed a most unusual sight.

A circle of khaki-clad GIs clustered around one of the new replacements. In one hand the soldier was hefting a big, mean-looking bullwhip made out of strips of braided black leather.

The guy with the bullwhip set up a line of empty glass bottles on a rotten palm log lying on the ground. To one side, another GI was taking bets on how many bottles he could shatter in a row and how fast he could shatter them.

Once the guy holding the bets had collected the cash, he borrowed a stopwatch and held up his hand.

"Ready, set . . . *go!*" he shouted out.

The guy with the bullwhip reared back and exploded into action. Onlookers differed about what happened next, because the action unfolded so quickly that it appeared to witnesses only as a blur of speed and motion.

Somehow in the next seconds the GI brandishing the bullwhip managed to smash every one of the bottles on the log to little pieces. The guy holding the stopwatch timed how long it took to accomplish this feat. It had taken the whip man only six seconds flat to smash the twenty bottles he'd set out in a line.

The GI onlookers were amazed and dumbfounded by the performance. They had hardly seen him move!

The other new replacement was a man of talents that were every bit as unique as those of the whip man, although his were talents of another sort entirely. Scully watched as the GI, having stripped to the waist, used a stick to draw a line in the dirt in front of him. Tossing aside the stick, he issued a challenge to all comers.

"I'll pay any man a C-note who can budge me from this here line," he shouted, holding up a one-hundred dollar bill. "That's right, you eggsuckers. A brand-new C-note to make all your dirty dreams come true next time you're on furlough."

Right away Pee Wee Drummond thought that he could make himself some easy money. The huge man from East Los Angeles didn't know what the challenger had up his sleeve, but to Pee Wee he looked like a runt and a piss-ant. No piss-ant runt who ever drew breath could give Pee Wee any trouble.

He'd fought the best contenders on the Los-Angeles-to-New-York wrestling circuit, facing contenders like Killer Kalamazoo Kurtz, Juma the Borneo Wild Man and Mad Mario the Masked Mexican Marauder. Living legends of the wrestling world, every damned one of them.

"One side," Pee Wee growled as he elbowed his way through the crowd surrounding the guy in the center who was holding up the long green note with the picture of the dead president in its center. Towering over the man, Pee Wee glared down at him. "You sure you want to try this?"

"Sure thing, sport," the dogface answered without a moment's hesitation. Pee Wee looked a little more closely and a little more carefully. The guy looked almost like a Mexican, he thought. His eyes were on the slanty side, though, almost slanty enough to be an Oriental. The runt had the muscular look of a guy who worked out and took care of himself. But he was still a runt, and that was all that counted as far as Pee Wee was concerned.

"Okay, Mac, I hope your plot's paid for," Pee Wee growled, then without further ado lunged for the man in front of him. But by the time his hand reached his intended target, the man wasn't standing there anymore.

Instead, he was tumbling between Pee Wee's legs, then he dodged to one side. It was almost as if he had walked right through him. In moments the massive man found himself spinning through the air end-over-end to land on his back with a resounding thud.

Pee Wee shook his head to clear it of the webs spun by invisible spiders that now hung before his eyes. Everything was swimming around on top of that. The sound of the laughing GIs encircling him enraged him to a red-hot fury. Heaving himself to his feet, Pee Wee launched a savage left-and-right combination at the smaller man.

But none of his blows landed at all. Instead, the smaller man was beckoning Pee Wee to charge him with a broad smile on his face. The taunting smile infuriated Pee Wee even more.

Lowering his head, Pee Wee charged. He was going for a pulverizing stomach butt that would settle the little guy's hash once and for all. But his opponent slipped Pee Wee's charge as expertly as he had neutralized Pee Wee's blows. Again Pee Wee found himself crashing to the ground, the wind knocked out of him.

"All right, break it up, you ding-a-lings!" Scully shouted, wading into the crowd and getting between the fuming Pee Wee and his smiling opponent, who had hardly broken a sweat and was still standing behind the line he'd drawn in the dirt. "Party time's over. Any more of this crap and you two bozos are both gonna spend the rest of the war peelin' potatoes and swabbin' out latrines. Am I makin' myself clear?"

"Yeah, Sarge," Pee Wee said sheepishly, although he still glared daggers at the man who had humiliated him in front of the whole platoon.

"Sorry, Sarge," the little guy answered. "I apologize. It was all my fault."

"Damned right it was," Scully shot back immediately. "Now, just who in Sam Hill are you, anyway?"

"My name's Private Sam Melendez, but most people call me 'Judo,' it's easier to say. I'm one of the guys who's supposed to replace some personnel that your unit lost." By then the other showman with the bullwhip had come over to join him, and he introduced himself as Private Smitty Hargett.

"Smitty and me are the only two guys who made it from our unit, which was First Platoon. We got hammered real hard by the Japs when we landed," Judo explained. He added that he was formerly the unit's scout and claimed to be a damned good one, too.

"Okay," Scully said, then lifted his hand warningly into the air. "Now, let's get one thing straight. No bellyachers, prima donnas or section eights are allowed in this unit. As far as you new men go, you get treated the same as the rest of us.

"We fight as a team. It's all for one and one for all, just like the three musketeers. Any more carryin' on like this, I'll see that both of you get court-martialed. I hope you guys read me."

"Loud and clear, Sarge," Judo and Hargett said promptly. The riot act having been read to the new men, Scully and the two replacements shook hands, then made them trade grips with Pee Wee. Shouting at the crowd once peace was made, Scully then dispersed the dogfaces. But he made up his mind to keep his eye glued on those two goldbricks just the same. Although he was pleased they were seasoned fighting men and not greenhorns, they looked like trouble.

SCULLY PRESENTED himself to Lieutenant Bloodworth in his administrative area—usually referred to by the GIs as the orderly room—in the commandeered outpost to receive his next set of orders.

"Scully, I want you to take your men on long-range patrol," Bloodworth informed the sergeant. He used his fingertip to point out an area of mountainous jungle country to the south of their position. According to the map, the sector was code-named Able Baker.

Bloodworth ran down a timetable for Scully, and they discussed recognition codes for radio transmissions, as well as times that the unit would report in to the CP. Scully saluted smartly and walked out of the orderly room.

He found his men billeted in their barracks, which had been cleared of all traces of the former occupants, and he relayed the bad news once he had called the whole unit to attention.

"Looks like we just hit the jackpot," Scully told them.

"Whaddaya mean, Sarge?"

"The sarge means we got the shit stick," somebody piped up. "Ain't that right, Sarge?"

"That's right," Scully answered with a nod, and then outlined their new assignment.

After the customary griping, cussing and grumbling, the men of the 160th packed their gear. Despite the show, they were professional soldiers who had been baptized by blood and steel. The following morning they would move out and start doing the job they had been trained to perform.

10

The platoon set off early in the morning and was soon deep into the dense jungle that lay to the south of their encampment. The island of Luzon was no mere rock in the Pacific. Roughly comparable in land mass, and even in shape, to the British Isles, there was enough terrain here so that a military patrol could easily be gone for a week. The men had drawn their supplies and ordnance with just such an eventuality in mind.

Acting as the unit's scout, Judo was on point. The wiry man seemed to be right at home in the jungle, moving with catlike grace, wasting no excessive motion nor taking a single misstep as he walked sure-footedly along.

Avoiding the roads whenever possible in order to decrease the threat of walking right into an ambush, and crossing them at a run when they had to, the column of dogfaces trudged through the jungle, using machetes to hack a path when needed. They were equipped with olive-drab oilskin ponchos, and on their first day out were grateful to have them when they found themselves inundated by a sudden tropical rainstorm.

The GI column walked out of the jungle while the storm was still raging around them, turning the ground into a sucking quagmire of mud crisscrossed by small rivulets of rainwater. Before long, Judo held up his hand in a signal for the unit to halt. The men at the front of the column could see why they stopped in a few moments. Up ahead were what appeared to be the shattered ruins of an old church.

Judo broke from the jungle cover and moved stealthily across the ground through gray sheets of rain. Alert-eyed and duck-walking at a half crouch, he made his way confidently toward the site of the ruins. A few minutes later he returned and advised Scully that the coast seemed clear. Their eyes wary, their bodies tense, the men filed out of the rain-deluged jungle without speaking and padded into the ruins of the church. Guards were set on the perimeter of the ruins, and they rested and prepared to wait out the storm.

WHEN THE RAINSTORM had finally moved on its course, Scully had Sparks call up the company's command post and briefly reported the platoon's position. Then the unit fell out again and penetrated deeper into the Able-Baker sector.

The region appeared to be a wasteland devoid of human life, and that fact was not altogether surprising. The Japanese occupation forces had been driven deeper and deeper into the interior of the vast island by the steadily advancing U.S. forces. The enemy had come as conquerors, not colonizers, and had not dug in to stay.

The Japanese employed a policy of scorched earth as standard military procedure. Indigenous populations were either used as slave labor or killed outright in what often became a policy of mass slaughter. Buildings were routinely razed to the ground or blown up so that the enemy invaders from America couldn't use them for billeting troops or as ready-made command posts.

After the platoon marched through even denser vegetation, the jungle began to thin out again. The brush tapered off and eventually gave way to an area of marshy bog country. The route of the patrol unit's advance led directly across the swampland. Scully didn't like the idea of crossing the large bog, where they would be exposed, and neither did Judo. The bog was a good place for planting hidden antipersonnel devices, and the man-high reeds and stands of *kunai* grass presented excellent blinds where enemy troops could lie in wait and not be detected until they were right on top of them.

"Fall in behind Melendez," Scully said to his troops as they emerged from the mangrove fringe of the bog land. "Wait till he gives the all clear." Scully detailed which men were to go and had them wait while Judo set about gathering sticks and sharpening the points with his bayonet knife. When he had gathered an armful, Judo slung his rifle over his shoulder and set off to cross the bog.

Moving swiftly and surely, Judo walked with his entire concentration riveted on the muddy bottom of the foul-smelling bog, alert for any minute telltale sign. The vegetation-choked water was murky, but he hoped he could spot clues to the presence of trip wires or other signs of disturbances in the natural pattern made by plants and water.

As Judo proceeded along, he struck the sharpened sticks into the bottom at intervals of every few feet. These would serve as guideposts for the rest of the squad to follow on its crossing of the bog. A few minutes later he reached the opposite bank and signaled with a wave that all was clear.

"Get going," Scully shouted at Applebaum, who was first in line. "And look alive."

Applebaum set off and reached the opposite bank of the marsh minutes later. Hargett, then Eightball, then Jacek went next while Scully kept his eye trained on the surrounding jungle terrain just in case the enemy happened to have ringside seats in the grass for the show.

Duke Osborne had become overconfident after he saw everybody make the crossing safely. He walked jauntily along with his Garand propped crosswise on his shoulders and his elbows in the air in front of him.

The monotony of the march had begun to make his mind wander, and he was thinking about his girl.

Halfway across the marsh, his boot slid off a slippery rock, and he stumbled six inches out of the path of safety that Judo had carefully marked out with the sticks in the muddy bottom. As he slipped, his left foot came down on the detonator stud of a Japanese antipersonnel mine, a type known as the bouncing betty.

The spring-loaded mine was a favorite booby trap deployed by the Japanese on Luzon as elsewhere in the Pacific, due to its natural suitability to emplacement in swamps, marshes and bogs. Osborne wasn't even aware that he had triggered the antipersonnel munition until it was too late for the knowledge to do him any good.

Detonating at Osborne's belt line, the high-explosive charge ripped through his abdominal region with a jagged spate of lethal shrapnel fragments. The explosion nearly tore Osborne in half. Not yet dead, he collapsed with a sodden splash into the bog's brackish waters, which quickly became tinged with his own blood.

Almost simultaneously the snipers who had been watching from concealed positions on either side of the marsh opened up with high-powered automatic rifles. As dogfaces on either bank of the marsh dropped for cover into the protection of the tall grass, the GI about to make dry land clutched his chest and flopped into the weed-choked water to lie flat on his face, his floating arms outstretched and limp.

The men directly behind Osborne hunkered down reflexively, as if trying to dip below the line of fire, and ran back toward the reed-lined shore. Heedless of any other booby traps that might lie in his path, Pee Wee tried to drag Osborne back toward shore, but enemy fire cut him off and he was forced to run back for cover.

"Help me! Somebody help me!" Osborne shouted out from where he lay leaking out his life in the middle of the marsh.

"Nobody move an inch," Scully commanded the troops flat on their bellies to the left and the right of him. "That's just what the Japs want us to do. As soon as we show ourselves, they'll pick us off like clay pigeons in a shooting gallery."

Again Osborne cried out for help. In the lull in the shooting that fell over the ambush ground, his pathetic pleas echoed across the fetid bog and were blown by the wind into the jungle beyond.

"Sarge, we gotta do something," Pee Wee implored. "We can't just let him lie there."

"What you gotta do, and the *only* thing you gotta do, is obey orders, Pee Wee," Scully grated at the GI. "Now, all of you—keep your heads down. I want a volunteer to see if we can circle around and take out one of the Japs. Who's got the guts?"

"I'm your man, Sarge," Smitty Hargett volunteered in an instant.

"Good man. Now, watch out for the rest of our guys on the other side," Scully warned him. "They may be trying to do the same thing we are. Make sure we don't wind up shooting at each other."

Quickly checking their weapons, the sergeant and Hargett made their way cautiously through the wind-blown reeds.

11

On the marshy bank opposite Scully's position, Judo instructed the four other GIs to keep their heads down and to distract the snipers in the rushes with answering fire. Then he took off to stalk the snipers and attempt to pinpoint their positions and devise a plan to neutralize them.

Moving stealthily through the tangled masses of man-high swamp grass, Judo left his position of concealment, mentally trying to fix its location in the anonymous sea of parched brown grass and rustling reeds. Now he could hear the coughing of the Japanese sniper rifles trading fire with the rest of his own detail back on the other side of the bog. The Japanese rifles had a distinctive-sounding report, while the American guns were clearly distinguished by their own particular accents.

Judo relied on the sounds that the weapons of the Japanese produced to pinpoint their locations. Listening carefully, using his ears like radar dishes, he sensed that the nearest sniper was positioned roughly five hundred feet from his position. The sniper was depending on the high swamp grass to provide effective cover as he cranked off one shot after another.

Standing stock-still, Judo watched for the telltale sign of muzzle-flash to alert him to the location of the sniper. From volley to volley, the flash of the Japanese gun changed position.

Judo had left his Garand in the safekeeping of the other members of the platoon. The job that needed doing now was better taken care of without the encumbrance of carrying a long-barreled weapon. All the weaponry that Judo required to take out the sniper he had at his disposal. His hands, feet, body and mind. *Those* were the only things he needed.

For that he had Mr. Suzuki to thank. Judo Melendez had started out as a sickly, skinny boy living in one of the barrios of Los Angeles. One day after he had been beaten by a gang of older toughs and lay dazed and bleeding on the sidewalk, Mr. Suzuki had come along, picked him up and tended to his wounds.

But he did more. Under his tutelage, Judo acquired the ancient Japanese martial arts of jujitsu and karate, learning to use his body and brain as the most potent weapons at his disposal.

Those skills served Judo well, and he had a special place in his heart for that kind and good man. Mr. Suzuki was also a true American citizen who did not agree with Japanese policies and approved Judo's role in the war effort.

The jungles of Luzon and the Japanese tactics offered Judo many a chance to make use of his special skills. The situation the platoon was now facing called

on his abilities, and he quickly ran through the possibilities in his mind.

The next time the sniper fired, Judo could clearly
detect the muzzle-flash of the powerful automatic rifle. It originated not more than a hundred feet from
his position. Movement beyond the edge of the jungle caught his eye. A figure was flitting through
patches of shadow cast by mangroves and palms.

The Japanese sniper.

Judo moved quickly, staking success if not survival
on the fact that the sniper was too intent on quickly
getting away from his last firing position before being
sighted and not expecting the unconventional approach Judo was using. His gamble paid off. In a few
minutes Judo managed to sneak up just behind and a
little to the right of the sniper, who had now again
gone to ground.

As he stood motionlessly in the swamp grass, Judo
used his eyes to scan the perimeter. There was no sign
of any backup. It was between him and the sniper. One
on one.

He could see the sniper clearly now, see the dull
black metal of his helmet and the khaki fabric of his
bush jacket beneath the fronds of giant ferns, the long
black barrel of his automatic rifle projecting from the
vegetation with cold, dark menace.

Picking up a rock lying nearby, Judo flipped it
deftly to one side of the sniper. The barrel of the rifle
instantly jerked to track the spinning, bouncing ob-

ject. For a split instant the barrel of the rifle pointed to one side, away from Judo's position.

Judo closed the distance separating him from his quarry in a second flat, moving with lightning speed. But the Japanese sniper was fast, too. As if realizing that he had been tricked by a diversion, he had turned away from the sudden sound and ended up directly facing Judo. Moving with surprising quickness, the sniper brought up the barrel of the rifle, swinging it to point at Judo as he triggered a round.

Judo's foot flashed in the air, and his toe caught the side of the barrel and knocked it aside a split instant before it spit out its deadly load. The round went wild and high as it was discharged, burrowing into the trunk of a mangrove tree several dozen yards away. Staggered by the powerful and accurate kick, the sniper lost his grip on the rifle with a howl of rage and pain and broke to one side to evade more of the same punishment.

Judo was surprised by the quickness of the maneuver. He recovered his balance on the follow-through of the kick, only to find that the sniper had drawn his sword and was running at him flat out, a battle cry on his lips.

The Japanese was fast, driven by fear and anger, and a capable fighter. The *Shin Gunto* sliced the air as it whipped in a glittering arc, chopping and swinging with precision. Dodging back and forth, rolling on his back among the matted-down grass, Judo heard the swishing of the sword blade as it whistled past his ear.

He was waiting for an opening, stalling his opponent with delaying tactics, and then he found what he was after. The razor-sharp blade of the samurai sword swung downward with great force and bit deep into the bark of the coconut palm next to Judo, and it took the enemy an extra second or two to free it. Judo used those fleeting seconds to grab the man's sword arm with one hand and deliver a punishing side-handed blow to the base of his throat.

His collarbone shattered, the sniper let go of the sword with an agonized shriek and fell spluttering and bleeding to the ground. But he hadn't given up, and even as he lay there writhing, he was already pulling a gun from side leather as Judo leapt high into the air.

A double thrust-kick delivered from midspring shattered the wrist and snapped the neck in quick succession. The sniper was taken out of the running for good. To complete the job, Judo pulled the sword from the tree in one swift motion, and then broke it by holding its tip down beneath his combat boot and pulling its handle sharply upward with all his might. Then he flung the two pieces to the ground beside the enemy's broken body.

A couple of minutes later Judo's buddies trained their weapons on the dim shape they had glimpsed moving toward them through the high cattails and grass of the marsh.

"Easy there, you birds, it's me," Judo said to them as he reached his buddies' position. Stooping, he retrieved his helmet, his rifle and his pack. "What about the other sniper?"

That question was answered as Sergeant Matt Scully and the rest of the veteran footsoldiers of Third Platoon came wading across the swamp toward them. Scully explained that the other sniper had taken off and melted back into the jungle as soon as the odds against him started getting long.

They had found his nest and spent shell casings, but the sniper himself was nowhere to be found, even after a thorough search of the surrounding area.

Fight and withdraw, fight and withdraw—that was the Japanese strategy in the Pacific islands. It was a strategy that each solitary warrior of the emperor employed, just as did higher organizational echelons right on up to the divisional level and beyond.

There was no chance that the men of Blackjack Company would manage to locate the sniper again.

"Let's shake it," Scully said, shouldering his weapon and eager to take leave of the barren place. "We've got a lot of ground to cover."

12

But before they moved out, there was one last grim chore to perform. Osborne and Longacre were dead. One had fallen at the sniper's hand, and the other had been the victim of the booby trap. The unit buried the two GIs far from home, in the lonely, godforsaken place where they had given their lives for their country. One of thousands of lonely, godforsaken places in the middle of nowhere where America's fighting men were dying all across the Pacific and Europe.

Papajohn and Finelli volunteered for the burial detail. The two men had been their buddies, and they felt it only right to pay them their last respects in this way. After they handed Scully the KIAs' personal effects and dog tags for Graves Registration when they got back to base, they jammed the KIAs' rifles muzzle-down into the muddy earth and propped their helmets over the buttstocks of their upended rifles. Papajohn said a brief and awkward eulogy over the makeshift graves.

But then it was time to move out again. They didn't look back at the forlorn graves of their dead buddies. When none of them knew which one would be next, or how soon, the only thing to do was to push on.

They couldn't stop to think about their chances because it would only work against them.

That seemingly callous attitude, characteristic of the infantry foot soldier, did not come about because the GI was hard or cruel or without human feeling. On the contrary, the dogfaces had formed bonds of friendship that had been forged by mutually shared danger and were stronger than any they had known in peacetime.

No, it wasn't lack of feeling that made them turn away from the fallen they had left behind. It was something else entirely. It was an attitude linked to the stark imminence of their own deaths in the jungle hellhole that made them turn away from the dying place toward the next mile of ground they had to slog across on their way to the next objective.

The living had yet to stop the proverbial bullet with their name on it. Somebody else had done it for them, this time around at least.

But each dogface who survived knew that he was as good as dead, as surely as the sun rose in the morning and set again at night. The infantry soldier understood that he was living on borrowed time, and every GI was aware of it with the same certainty he had when he remembered his own name.

In the end it came down to just this: the graves they had left behind were as good as their own graves, and none of them wanted to linger too long. Some of the dead lay resting in peace. Some of the other dead walked on. For the men of Third Platoon, it was the only distinction that mattered.

The GI column continued along its line of march. The patrol used the roads for a time, having grown sick and tired of hacking their way through dense jungle underbrush, their eyes alert to the slightest signs of enemy presence. Halting suddenly, Judo signaled for the platoon to stop. As they looked on, he bent low and put his ear to the roadbed.

"Sounds like some trucks are coming our way," he said to Scully when he straightened again. "I'm gonna climb a tree and have a look around."

Judo quickly shimmied up the trunk of a big coconut palm and held his field glasses up to his eyes. Through a shimmering haze of thermal distortion caused by the glare and heat of the intense tropical sun, he could discern the cause of the vibrations that he had heard in the roadbed.

The Japanese motorized patrol unit was made up of a scout car with a motorcycle escort. The patrol was coming down a gently sloping grade of the narrow mountain road that switchbacked between the steep vegetation-swathed hills.

Judo clambered down from the top of the palm tree with the agility of a monkey.

"Well?" Scully asked the private.

"Honorable Jap convoy coming down the road, Sarge." Judo then explained what he'd seen. Scully thought for a second and then spoke to the rest of the unit.

"You goofballs heard the man," he said. "Now get the lead out."

Hurriedly barking orders, Sergeant Matt Scully instructed Barrows to set up his Browning chattergun at a point where the road came out of a narrow hairpin turn and formed a straightaway between the flanking trees.

The way Scully figured it, the Browning would finish off the armored scout car while the motorcyclist could be taken out with a bomb trap activated by a taut-wire detonator. After he unshipped grenades from military webbing draped crosswise on his chest, Scully set about taping together four of the grenades to make a cluster charge.

When the preparation was complete, he tied a length of military-issue nylon cord to the cotter pin of one of the grenades and strung it across the roadbed at the approximate level of the scout bike's front fender.

Stepping back a few feet, Scully surveyed his handiwork with a practiced eye. The trip wire was invisible until you were right on it—he could tell at a glance. Scully was confident that the oncoming enemy were about to get the surprise of their lives—the last one, if he had his way.

The Japanese in the motorized patrol unit came rolling along just like clockwork. Two men rode in the armored vehicle, and in front was their escort on the motorcycle, which bore a small flag attached to its fender.

The column proceeded on confidently until the cyclist rode headlong into the trip wire. The grenade cluster charge rigged by Scully was triggered and blew just as the armored car was passing athwart it.

The force of the blast tore off the two big tires on the armored wagon's left side. Out of control, the armored vehicle careered wildly on the road, rending the air with the scream of fragmenting metal and tortured, shrieking tires, followed by an awful grating of bare wheel rims against earth and stone.

Scully's men discharged their rifles at the cyclist, setting up a wall of killfire, and Barrows cut loose with the Browning machine gun at the armored car.

A .30-caliber slug penetrated one of the gun ports in the armor-plate exterior of the wagon and struck the driver. As he sagged to one side, he let go of the steering wheel. The war wagon went completely out of control and skidded off the roadway, landing on its side in the drainage ditch with bare metal wheel rims spinning uselessly. Then a spark from somewhere caught on a fuel spill, and the armored wagon began to burn slowly, amid rising clouds of noxious gray-brown smoke.

Scully was already up and running toward the burning vehicle. As he reached it, he saw a bloody hand lift up the hatch of the Japanese armored car. Acting quickly, Scully stuck the muzzle of his tommy gun into one of the gunports and convulsively jerked the trigger, making the SMG buck in his fists as it chattered madly away, pumping the interior full of burning steel.

Scully was rewarded by the sound of a strangled moan coming from within the stricken vehicle. The fingers of the hand went stiff, and briefly clawed at the metal. Finally the bloodstained hand fell back lifelessly and the hatch closed with a dull metallic clang.

The GIs pulled the dead bodies from the wreckage. Scully searched them meticulously and found papers in a small leather map case. The military maps showed the location of a bridge and a troop garrison farther to the north.

Scully put the map case away with his own gear for safekeeping. Their discovery had the hallmarks of the kind of find that the Intelligence boys back at the base were anxious to get their hands on.

Then, at Scully's signal the platoon lobbed grenades at the wrecked vehicles. When the pineapples blew, the ruptured fuel lines caught fire completely, and the gas tanks blew with earsplitting bangs. The Japanese army would never use them against American forces again.

The unit struck out anew, leaving the ruined, burning vehicles behind them as grim reminders of war's savage price for the evil that men do.

13

The patrol moved on with Judo scouting ahead for telltale signs of enemy activity. The rest of the unit followed behind with Scully and Eightball bringing up the rear and Applebaum, Finelli and Mockler on the flanks.

They kept up the march for days, and the men were dog-tired, unshaven, foul smelling and empty bellied. They would have given their eyeteeth for hot food and the chance to shed their mud-encrusted uniforms and wash. But the likelihood of that happening anytime soon was remote. The patrol had a job to do, and until that job was completed, there would be none of the amenities that awaited them back at camp.

They were leaving a thickly rain-forested area and moving into a sizable open field of sun-parched *kunai* grass dotted with a few coconut palm groves when Applebaum let out a shout of alarm.

"Look alive! Jap spotter plane at three o'clock."

At once the patrol detail ducked for cover into a deep irrigation ditch half-covered with high *kunai* grass. The ditches crisscrossed the field, which had once been a copra plantation that had long since gone to seed.

The coconut palms from which the meaty nut had been harvested by the plantation workers had reverted to a wild state, and only a few of them remained standing. The many ditches were both a blessing and a curse, for the enemy could also rely on them for concealment and remain undetected until a GI was practically on top of them.

Still, it was very provident that the terrain afforded such a natural and valuable cover. Lying flat on their bellies in the abandoned irrigation ditches, the GIs of Blackjack Company's Third Platoon were all but invisible to the occasional observation aircraft that droned overhead.

Watching cautiously from their places of concealment, their bodies effectively camouflaged by the sea of waving *kunai* grass, they followed the flight of the low-flying scout plane for long minutes until it disappeared into the sun over the waving tops of the twenty-foot-high coconut palms.

Scully sounded the all clear when the last echoes of the plane's single engine faded into a distant background drone. The khaki-clad troops broke from cover, hitched their packs on their backs and shouldered their rifles. They stretched their limbs and paused to pop wads of cut plug tobacco into their mouths, then with some cussing and griping willed themselves into motion once again. The patrol moved out, vanishing in a khaki line from the bright sunlight into the shadows of dense jungle.

As THE SUN CLIMBED to its zenith in the clear blue sky, the patrol came to the burned-out remains of a Filipino village. The village had been pillaged by Japanese forces and was now completely desolate, another casualty of the war in the Pacific.

Every structure that had once stood there had been razed to the ground by the retreating enemy to ensure that the conquering American troops wouldn't derive any benefit from it. Not even a stray dog or barnyard animal could be seen amid the charred outlines in the dusty ground that marked the places where Filipino homes had housed men, women and children.

Third Platoon did not linger among the ruins. When no sign of the enemy was detected in the vicinity of the village, the platoon was ready to continue its march. The men averted their eyes as they moved out, their spirits dampened by the sorry sight. No one had the heart for the usual cracking of jokes. The wiped-out Filipino village had cast its black shadow on their hearts and minds, and every dogface was eager to put as much distance behind him as possible.

The jungle began to thin out as the patrol reached the extreme limits of Sector Able Baker. The sector map Scully carried in his field jacket identified the area as a factory zone. Formerly it had been devoted to processing the raw rubber that was traditionally harvested in the form of latex sap on the plantations dotting the district for many miles around.

With Judo acting as scout, the patrol unit began to move forward in a different manner. All cigarettes were quickly extinguished. Eventually, after they had left the plundered village behind, the men had resumed the usual gruff joking and bantering that helped them endure their lot.

Now they all fell silent again, filled with the foreboding that comes over a line platoon when the closeness of violent death is upon them. The faces were tense, with somber expressions. Their eyes were alive, darting from left to right, to the treetops and the ground, as they scanned with a narrow-eyed, anxious glance.

The platoon was registering the palpable presence of danger. They reacted to the promptings of a sixth sense that comes to a line soldier who has done his share of combat time. It is a sixth sense that is as reliable as radar, sonar or any other warning mechanism. Each GI was in the grip of this ancient, primitive warning system as he approached closer and closer to the factory zone.

CORPORAL SHITO was combing the area through his field glasses. He made a slow, lazy sweep, then his body stiffened. Through the powerful field glasses he had seen a flash of sudden motion through the sun-dappled perimeter of the rain forest edge. Patiently he kept the field glasses trained on the patch of jungle beyond the perimeter of the bomb-shattered factory building, and his diligence and patience were now rewarded by the first sighting of the enemy troops.

There was no mistaking the helmets or the khaki combat fatigues of the soldiers approaching the Imperial soldiers' position. They were American GIs. As Shito continued to scan the GI column, he was assured that the strength of the oncoming infantry force was no greater than a handful of men. That meant that he and his troops were only facing a patrol and not a company or battalion. Shito continued to watch until he was certain of his observation.

This Intelligence was good and yet bad at the same time. Shito's unit was one of many such details that had received orders to fall back into the concealment of the jungle. They had been instructed to engage the enemy in a series of guerrilla strikes that would decimate his numbers and harry his advance into the interior of Luzon.

Having sustained extremely high casualties during the course of the American invasions and the mop-up actions following the initial landing assaults, Shito's platoon had lost countless fully-blooded combat troops.

Many of the surviving fighting men were wounded, and they were woefully short on ammunition and supplies. Indeed, the unit depended on foraging parties for all their food and water, and the war-ravaged countryside was in short supply of both these staples.

It was fortunate, thought Corporal Shito, that the approaching adversary was roughly the same size as his own unit. On the other hand, death was an aspired honor for the soldiers of the emperor, and although his men might meet their deaths in an armed confrontation with these troops, they wouldn't be able to take five or six of the enemy with them.

Shito spoke quickly and mutedly into his walkie-talkie. Sound traveled by unaccustomed paths in the heat and stifling humidity of the subtropics. The portable radio unit connected him with his platoon commander, Lieutenant Katayama. At once the lieutenant commanded the Japanese platoon to engage the enemy and destroy it, and exhorted them to gladly embrace the prospects of the glorious deaths that the fortunate among them would meet.

14

The crack of a rifle round ripped through the desolate stillness a fraction of an instant after McGurk toppled with a ragged wound in his side. The rest of the unit dodged for cover, as though they were propelled by tightly coiled springs concealed within their uniforms.

Instantly they knew what had happened. *Sniper.*

"Muzzle-flash came from that window to the left on the factory building over there," Jacek remarked to Scully, his eyes glued to the sun-drenched brick facade broken by the yawning casements devoid of windowpanes. Here and there the scarred and weather-damaged interior of the gutted building shell was visible, exposed lath and plaster slatwork from caved-in walls and hanging electrical cables showing through the empty casements.

"I think I saw another one from a window over to the right on the ground level," observed Mockler.

"How's McGurk?" Scully asked, temporarily ripping his gaze from the factory shell.

Barrows was crouching over the downed private. McGurk looked as pale as a sheet, and his eyes were narrowed to slits. He gritted his teeth to suppress a moan. The agony that began as a dull, throbbing fire in his injured side had become an epicenter from which great, pounding waves of searing madness spread through his body in a ceaseless tide.

"Jeez, it hurts," McGurk groaned. "A-ah, it's a bitch."

"Looks to me like the bullet passed clean through," Barrows said as he tore open a packet of sulfa powder and sprinkled the white crystalline antibiotic compound on the ragged red wound. "But I don't know that for sure, Sarge. The slug might have hit a bone."

After applying the powder, Barrows procured a sterile gauze dressing from another first-aid packet and applied it to the wound. Then he got out a quarter-grain morphine Syrette from his first-aid kit. The Syrette was made up of a collapsible metal tube with a hypodermic needle attached to it, covered with a plastic tube. Breaking the seal on the plastic tube, he broke the seal on the metal tube containing the morphine to prepare the Syrette for injection.

Turning McGurk's arm over, he found a vein and jabbed the needle into the artery in a single quick motion, then squeezed the metal tube. The golden-brown liquid at first stung as it was slowly ejected from the needle and entered McGurk's bloodstream. But then the fire died down and along with it the tide of pain slowly ebbed and then receded.

McGurk took a deep breath and opened his eyes. "I'll be okay now," he said with a nod. "Just give me a couple of minutes." Barrows leaned McGurk up against a section of concrete wall and handed him a wad of cut plug chewing tobacco. Grabbing his helmet and his weapon, Barrows loped off to rejoin his buddies.

"I gave McGurk some morphine," he told Scully. "I think he'll be okay."

"Wish I could say that about the rest of us," Scully growled back in response. The enemy had opened up again with a fresh volley of rifle fire originating from the ruins of the factory shell. Now the platoon could plainly see that a machine-gun emplacement had been set up behind sandbags before a gutted section of the abandoned factory building.

Scully was fast on his feet. He had devised a mode of attack, and he gave orders intended to cope with the situation. He broke the unit up into three squads. Squad one, with Barrows and Papajohn cranking out slugs from the Browning machine gun, would provide cover for the assault. Squads two and three, led by himself and Mockler respectively, would circle around to try to take the factory ruins in a pincer movement.

As Barrows and Papajohn opened up with the Browning, Scully's and Mockler's teams moved in on the factory ruins. The building was large, and the Japanese soldiers inside were intent on holding out to the last man. They could be relied on to fight with the same fanatical devotion to wiping out the enemy forces that had marked the American's every encounter with the Japanese so far.

Coming in from left and right, the two teams faced immediate and fierce opposition. Two of the enemy attacked Eightball in a wild, screaming banzai charge. They ran at the Americans, firing their rifles from the hip, not giving a damn that they were placing themselves directly into the line of fire.

With his tommy gun Applebaum jabbed the head of a Japanese soldier. The man's jaw fractured with an audible crack, but he was still in the running. He raised the short sword he carried in his belt, and in a surprisingly quick and fluid motion that was almost impossible for the unpracticed eye to follow, thrust it straight into Applebaum's shoulder. Blood spurted from the wound in a sudden shower as a sick, hot pain stabbed through the GI's entire nervous system.

Applebaum lashed out with his booted foot, landing a blow in the groin area. Then he followed up with another swipe of the Garand's hefty buttstock. That double play sent the man to the ground in a heap.

Unscabbarding his long knife, Applebaum finished the job with two hard and deep stabs of the all-purpose GI dagger that he always made a point to keep well-honed and ready for action. Leaving his dirk embedded in the dead man, Applebaum hastily fashioned a tourniquet from his belt and applied it to his shoulder.

The wound was throbbing with a dull yet fierce pain, but with each moment that passed, it flared hotter and he was already beginning to grit his teeth against it. He realized that in a while the pain would flare up to the point where he might need to use one of the morphine Syrettes from his first-aid kit.

Tying the tourniquet tightly, he made up his mind to hold out against the pain for as long as he was able. He had heard of guys getting hooked on morphine and turning into junkies.

The thought of going back home as a drug addict horrified him. Addicts didn't live long, and they even stopped being interested in sex after a while. That low, Applebaum never wanted to sink. He finished tying off the wound, then repossessed his dagger and ported his rifle, fighting off the steadily building waves of pain.

The fighting wasn't over in the factory ruins. Corporal Mockler was pursing a couple of Japanese soldiers through the levels of the abandoned structure. All of a sudden, as he ran beneath an archway separating one big room from another, one of them wheeled around and the rifle in his fists barked twice in quick succession. His partner whipped a potato masher grenade from a musette bag at his side and tossed it at Mockler, who had ducked sideways behind the cover of a vertical I-beam support.

Sprinting from cover as fire spanged off the steel beam, Mockler managed to snatch up the grenade as it rolled toward him. He tossed it back into the shadowy recesses ahead of him.

Almost as soon as the grenade struck the deck, it exploded with a loud, sharp bang that was magnified and intensified by the acoustics of the gutted factory interior. The fragmenting submunition sent a choking, billowing dust cloud of pulverized concrete and plasterwork spewing in Mockler's direction.

He ported the Garand he carried and fired straight into the eye-stinging dust cloud. He was firing the repeating rifle blind, not knowing whether he had hit the enemy at all as he heard the ricochets of the .30-caliber automatic striking concrete. He fired a few more short bursts as the dust cleared, and then looked cautiously around.

The two soldiers were sprawled in positions of death, he saw to his relief. One of them was draped over empty metal hoppers with half his face missing.

His companion also appeared dead, lying facedown on the concrete floor, his legs scissored behind him. Mockler let the still-smoking Garand fall to his side and turned the body over with the steel toe of his combat boot.

As the "corpse" rolled over, he saw that the hand held a small black automatic pistol. But it was too late for him to act. With a belch of hot yellow flame, the pistol went off at almost point-blank range and nearly blinded him with the intense flash from its muzzle. His ears rang from the report, and he felt a terrible heat spread across his face.

Enveloped in the red haze of battle and acting purely on reflex, Mockler brought up the muzzle of the Garand before another bullet could be fired at him, and squeezed the trigger until the clip of .30-caliber rounds was completely empty.

Each bark of the repeating-fire weapon found its mark in the Japanese soldier. The body was riddled through and through, and even after all life had gone out of it, continued twitching on the concrete floor. Long after the Garand had run dry of ammunition, Mockler stood squeezing the trigger, still seeing the enemy coming at him and not realizing that the fight was over. Then he stood panting, the adrenaline still pumping through his system, feeling as though he had gone to the limits of sanity and back.

15

The dead bodies of many of the Japanese defenders were piled up already on the killing ground before the ruined factory. Barrows picked up the Browning MG and ran toward the building, cradling the chattering automatic weapon in his brawny, tattooed arms. Backing him up was Papajohn, the clip-fed Thompson SMG in his fists ejecting .45-caliber rounds from its muzzle at a cycling rate of 800 rounds per minute.

The big .30-caliber machine gun chattered a deep basso to the tommy's high-pitched contralto as the GIs belted out their murderous duet in the face of determined opposition. Under their relentless barrage, as well as the ground-clearing effect of pitched grenades, the Japanese continued falling. Pouring on the steam, the two blasted and charged their way into the humid interior of the factory's shadowed ground level, and their boots crunched over chunks of debris littering the shattered floor.

From the next level above them, Barrows and Papajohn could hear the sound of sporadic automatic fire and the cursing and yelling of men locked in combat. Despite the high toll of enemy forces killed and wounded in the engagement thus far, the fight was plainly far from over yet. The Japanese were fighting as though they were men possessed, their ancient feudal codes of honor barring surrender. Both sides knew that neither of them could afford to give or take any quarter.

Scully and Private Biff Mahoney found themselves face-to-face as they converged from opposite ends of a dogleg corridor. Pumped full of adrenaline, the GIs had been a trigger-squeeze away from death.

Each GI had rounded the corridor's bend figuring that the other one was surely the enemy. They had faced each other with muzzles raised and fingers tight on the triggers. It was sheer luck that saved them: a second or two earlier or later, and they might have blown each other away in the heat of action.

"Holy cow," Mahoney said as together they pressed forward from the debris-choked corridor into an adjoining chamber. Iron rails set into the concrete floor suggested that it had housed heavy machinery, but it was bare of anything except empty oil drums and packing crates lying in heaps everywhere. "Good thing it's you, Sarge. I thought I had me a Jap on the other side for sure."

The words were hardly out of his mouth when the hot, foul-smelling air exploded with a tumultuous burst of rapidly cycling automatic fire. A Japanese officer with a machine pistol had appeared from out of nowhere, darting from behind a section of half-collapsed wall. The surprise burst caught Mahoney squarely across the lower body, destroying his life, letting his blood stream away in a crimson river.

Uttering the single syllable *"No!"* Mahoney toppled with his arms reflexively reaching back to break his fall. But he was already gone, save for the twitching muscles set into motion by his screaming nervous system. He came down with a crash against an empty steel drum, throwing it over in the process. With a mournful crash the toppled drum and his body rolled in opposite directions before both finally came to rest.

The officer raised the machine pistol to fire another autoburst at Scully, but the tough and combat-hardened sergeant was too fast. Snatching up the steel lid from one of the empty drums nearby, he used it as a makeshift though effective shield against enemy fire. Firing the tommy from the hip, Scully forced his attacker to duck, and the shot from the subgun went wild and high. The improvised defensive maneuver bought Scully enough breathing time to dodge behind a packing crate.

Ejecting the spent drum magazine of .45-caliber rounds from the Thompson's receiver and ditching it, Scully got an interchangeable standard box magazine out of a canvas pouch on his web utility belt and snapped it smartly into the receiver. Pulling back the cocking lever of the Thompson in one smooth and well-practiced motion, he chambered a fresh round and waited for the other man to make his play.

But no sound came from the abandoned storeroom beyond his place of cover. Scully saw the sunlight filtering dustily through glassless casement windows and heard the rustling of the palms from outside and the pop-pop-pop of sudden gunfire accompanied by shouting in English and Japanese. But from directly in front of him there was nothing. No sound, no movement.

Why didn't the Jap make a move? Scully asked himself as he crouched there. As he waited motionlessly, sweat started to ooze from his pores. What the hell was he waiting for? Scully wondered. A droplet of sweat rolled down his forehead from under the lip of his helmet and fell into his eyes, stinging him for a moment.

He raised his sleeve to wipe the sweat from his eyes and just as he did so, the enemy made his play. With a suddenness that made Scully jump, a volley of SMG fire raked the crate behind which Scully hunkered. Jagged chips of wood, sharp as razor blades, bit into the flesh of his skin as the evil mosquito whine of ricocheting bullets flew at him.

Reacting instantly, Scully jumped from cover. The tommy was on fire in his fists as he ran, zigzagging toward the officer who stood in the doorway across the room, belching out its staccato sound of vengeance as he slapped shoe leather against concrete and hurled his body through space with the fury that only a man fighting for his life can muster.

Taken aback by the fury of Scully's charge, the man ducked back into a smaller side-chamber beyond the doorway. Scully had been fast, though, and some of the tommy's .45-caliber bullets had stitched him across his shoulder before he could get completely out of sight.

Hit by the tommy burst, the officer went down for the count, spattering the gutted wall and the packing crates strewn behind him with dark red nickel-sized droplets of suddenly spilled blood. Weakened and moaning with pain, he raised his pistol to fire at Scully, but the sergeant had already clamped the sole of his boot down on the gun hand.

Scully realized then, as he took a good look, that the man was an officer. Therefore he would make good prisoner material. Scully made him sit up and disarmed him swiftly, looking around to make sure there was no backup lurking in the shadows. The Japanese officer grimaced but otherwise said nothing, even though his shoulder was wounded and the left side of his uniform was completely soaked through with blood.

"Alright, Tojo," Scully growled then, sticking the muzzle of the tommy in the small of his captive's back when he was finished checking the perimeter. "Lead the way and don't try nothin' funny." Scully intended to radio back to base for instructions. The patrol had been instructed to take no prisoners, but he had a feeling that the boys from G-2 might want to question the captured enemy officer just the same.

THERE WAS ONE OTHER prisoner left alive once the factory building was taken. Scully's men could get nothing out of either of the prisoners, although it

wouldn't have helped much even if they were talka-
tive because none of them talked Japanese, save for a
few words of pidgin.

Sending Eightball, Mockler and Hargett out to
scout for any other Japanese who might be hiding out
in the area, Scully radioed back to base to report that
they had taken two prisoners. He wasn't surprised
when he heard the negative response. They had been
sent out with orders to take no prisoners and that
meant only one thing.

The faces of the GIs were long when they heard the
news. They couldn't leave the prisoners alive, but just
the same, they weren't cold-blooded murderers. Killing an enemy soldier in the heat of action was one
thing. Shooting him dead in cold blood was an entirely different matter.

Suddenly the Japanese officer decided the issue for
the whole platoon. Unexpectedly he grabbed Papajohn and hauled the GI before himself. Quickly he
whipped the .45 from the GI's holster and held the
muzzle up against his head.

"I speak English," he informed them with a snarl
of hatred and contempt. "Throw down your weapons now. You are all prisoners of the Imperial army."

At that moment Scully came running up. This was
the same officer that he had gone up against before.
Although he was wounded, he was otherwise intact.
The way Scully sized up the situation, the man must
have heard the radio transmission and figured that he
had nothing to lose.

"Forget about it, pal," Scully said. "The play won't work. Put down the gun, nice and easy."

"I give the orders here!" the officer said hoarsely. His manner suggested a man used to brooking no dissent. "I give you five seconds, then I will shoot this enlisted man. Do you want that, Sergeant? Do you want this man's blood on your hands?"

"Don't listen to him, Sarge," Papajohn shouted. Scully could see that his eyes were wide with fear and that he was swallowing hard. They were brave words, but even Papajohn didn't mean them.

"Okay, you win, Tojo," Scully said, laying down his tommy gun. "It's just like you say."

"But, Sarge—" Papajohn began.

"But nothing, soldier," Scully shouted. "I give the orders around here." Scully slowly advanc.d on the officer. Handing over his .45, butt-end first, his eyes dark and hard, he said, "Here it is."

As the officer reached out to take hold of the weapon and stuff it in his belt, momentarily exposing his left side, Scully whipped out a second gun he had concealed behind his back and shot him right through the heart.

As if propelled by the force of the bullet, the officer toppled sideways, dropping his gun, and kicked out his feet and arms, finally rolling over on his back. His eyes took on a faraway look before they glazed over completely and went dark and icy cold, as though fires inside them had been extinguished forever. For a moment Scully thought that the man was trying to smile at him as a death grimace pulled up the corners of his mouth.

"Hey, Sarge," Applebaum shouted out suddenly, "the other Jap, he ain't here anymore."

Their other prisoner was gone. A few minutes before, he had been waiting there with frightened eyes. Scully figured he had run into the jungle when the attention of the GIs was focused on the officer's escape bid.

"You want us to go look for him?" Applebaum continued, his eyes scanning the jungle periphery. "Huh, Sarge, you want us to?"

"You do whatever you want," Scully growled in answer, sitting down and lighting up a Lucky Strike. "You just go follow your nose, Applebaum," he said with sudden disgust, and for the moment let the war and all its dehumanizing horror go away from him as he inhaled deep into his lungs and turned his gaze up toward the blazing disk of the sun in the heartbreakingly clear and beautiful tropical skies and stared hard at it, without blinking, for a very long time.

BOOK TWO:
Hard Earned Glory

16

Back at the base Second Platoon now had its hands full. After massing in the jungle, the Japanese had counterattacked at nightfall in a raw-steel banzai charge that was planned as a desperate and fierce attempt to take back their outpost. But the charge, like the ones that had preceded it, had been repulsed by Lieutenant Bloodworth's Blackjack Company.

When Scully's crew returned from its sector patrol, the men found the aftermath of the night attack still in the mop-up stages. Bodies of the fallen, Japanese and American alike, were being loaded into the trucks sent by Graves Registration. In the field hospital, men lay packed together like sardines in a can. Casualties were spilling over into the base compound due to the high cost in men and matériel of defending and holding the secured position.

The mood of the servicemen was anything but grim, however. Third Platoon found those who were not directly engaged in the unpleasant tasks that went with cleaning up after the pitched battle to be in high spirits.

Sunshine Division infantrymen sat in little groups around the encampment. They were busy with a variety of maintenance tasks—oiling bayonets freshly sharpened on a whetstone or loading machine-gun belts with .30-caliber rounds or expertly fieldstripping their service rifles to thoroughly clean and oil the taken-down parts.

Applebaum happened upon one such GI with whom he was acquainted as he passed beneath one of the tall coconut palms in a small grove situated on the camp perimeter.

"Hey, Applebaum," a voice cried from the topmost fronds of the tree that formed a broad-leafed canopy high above the head of the passing dogface. "Is that you down there, Applebaum?"

Startled, the private looked up toward the source of the voice, shading his eyes from the intense glare of the fierce near-equatorial sun. He found that he was unable to see anything distinctly except for the signs of movement up above in the rustling bower of giant tropical leaves. "You got the right name there, pal," he shouted back up toward the treetop. "Now, just who are you?"

"It's me, O'Leary," the voice drifted down, and at last Applebaum recognized the voice of private Ray O'Leary, lately of West Los Angeles and more lately of Guadalcanal and New Britain.

"Gangway, Applebaum," O'Leary's disembodied voice continued a moment later, "load of grade-A coconuts coming right at you."

O'Leary used his razor-edged machete to hack all the way through the tough stalk that secured a cluster of about fifteen green coconuts to the top of the palm tree. Applebaum stepped back just in the nick of time as the coconut bunch hit the ground at his feet, thudding into the organic litter of the forest floor with a loud whumping sound. O'Leary came clambering down with great agility only moments later, his scabbarded machete clacking against the trunk of the tree as he descended.

"Japs hit us with everything they had just after midnight," O'Leary explained as he expertly used the machete to hack a hole in a green, tough-rinded coconut. "They came out of nowhere in one banzai charge after another. Wave after wave of the bastards. You should oughta have seen it, Applebaum. I tell you, it could give a man gray hair overnight."

Applebaum tipped back the coconut and allowed the sweet, musky-tasting milk to splash against the roof of his mouth and trickle lazily and slowly down his throat. With water stores as scarce on Luzon as they were elsewhere in the Pacific Islands, coconut milk was the next best thing to a reliable supply of drinking water. After a while the GI developed a taste for both the saplike milk and the chewy, fibrous meat, and didn't even notice that it wasn't exactly a Coke or Pepsi he was gulping down or a mouthful of hamburger he was munching.

"Lot of casualties?" Applebaum asked, draining the coconut of its last quenching drops of milk.

"More of the Japs than us," O'Leary returned resolutely. "But a couple of guys I think you know got their clocks punched. Billy Gutzwiller from the San Fernando Valley and Harry Thompson.''

"What say we have a drink to them both, O'Leary," Applebaum suggested, but his expression had soured. Like other combat veterans, he didn't like to display his feelings of loss, but they went deep. So instead, both he and O'Leary cut open fresh green coconuts and drained their contents as they sat upon the very ground that had soaked in the blood from men's veins during the deadly hours of the war-torn night.

SCULLY AND HIS PATROL were immediately debriefed by Lieutenant Bloodworth. The debriefing was conducted in the lieutenant's orderly room where a big tactical map hanging on the wall depicted the various sectors that comprised Blackjack Company's area of operations.

Scully had the sector map he had carried with him already memorized and pointed out without any difficulty the many different aspects of the patrol's movements through Sector Able Baker. The sergeant detailed the encounter with Japanese snipers in crossing the bog and the engagement with the platoon at the abandoned rubber refinery building complex.

Having answered Bloodworth's questions, Scully produced the worn leather map case that he had taken from the Japanese officer after the ambush Third Platoon had set for the enemy mechanized patrol. Bloodworth briefly scanned the ideogram-covered documents and maps inside the pouch, declared them interesting and immediately called in an aide to dispatch the documents to the company translator.

Bloodworth shook Scully's hand and dismissed the sergeant and his men with a brisk thanks for a job well done. After the debriefing the sergeant figured that he needed a drink and proceeded to rustle one up, having noticed that a ramshackle canteen had been rigged up in his absence. On the way to imbibe his justly deserved refreshment, Scully passed Applebaum and O'Leary, who offered the NCO a swig of coconut milk.

"Better grab one of these babies while you can, Sarge," Applebaum shouted at Scully. "They're goin' pretty fast."

"Nix on that action," Scully told them, and walked on past the two dogfaces squatting on the ground as though they were having some kind of powwow. Scully wanted to have a drink, all right, but coconut milk was most definitely not the type of beverage he had in mind.

It wasn't long before the sergeant ran into Eightball and Jacek, who, he suddenly realized with pleasure, had exactly the type of medicine he needed to cure what ailed him. "How about that stash of jungle juice we found just after we landed?" he asked the two enlisted men. Scully figured there would have to be more of the stuff hidden in the woods somewhere—if he knew the men in his platoon, that is.

"We were just on our way to get some, Sarge," the enlisted men replied to Scully with broad grins on their tanned faces.

After a brief trek through tangled underbrush into the jungle at the periphery of the encampment, the three dogfaces were soon busying themselves with uncovering the two earthen jugs of the white lightning that they had not turned over after the original discovery of the cache of home brew. Uncorking one of the big jugs, the three GIs passed around the Imperial army home brew and were soon pleasantly intoxicated.

Jacek was getting drunker faster than his two buddies. The more he drank, the more he started thinking about his girlfriend, Annabell. He knew that she was hot stuff, and he had never believed her promise to be faithful until he came back home to the States. Annabell couldn't help herself, he knew darned well. She worked as a dance-hall girl and was constantly getting propositioned by guys.

"Still, she oughta have respect," Jacek slurred.

"What the hell you jabbering about, Jacek?" asked Scully and Eightball, who were rapidly catching up to his inebriated state.

"Annabell, thass who I'm talkin' about," Jacek rambled on in his drunken stupor. In his mind he could see her giving some smooth guy the time, just the way she used to give him the time a couple of times a day. Annabell was always giving the time. She was that kind of a dame. Now Jacek was convinced she was two-timing him.

His head became heavier and heavier, and with Annabell still on his mind, he started nodding off. Just then, Scully caught a glimpse of something moving in the bushes. Looking up suddenly, he gaped as he saw one of the biggest-looking pythons in the world slithering straight for him. Giving out a startled yelp, Scully jumped up. Eightball also caught sight of the huge snake, scrambled to his feet and began hacking the snake to pieces with the machete he carried.

"She's giving some damn gigolo the time right now, I betcha," Jacek kept muttering on, not even noticing the snake through the alcoholic haze in his brain. Having dispatched the reptilian interloper, Scully and Eightball grabbed the babbling GI and took him back to the camp compound, making sure to bring their cache of Japanese spirits along.

17

After a couple of days of rest Scully found himself and his troops handed a brand-new, shiny and highly dangerous assignment by his commanding officer, Lieutenant Bloodworth.

When Scully walked in, Bloodworth was sitting behind his desk, contemplatively puffing on a briar pipe, one of several that were arranged neatly on a pipe rack sitting atop his desk. There was a newcomer in the orderly room, too, Scully noticed. Gray-haired, the newcomer wore the same bar as did Bloodworth.

"Sergeant," Bloodworth began without further ado the moment Scully had shut the door behind him and stepped into the room. "I would like you to meet Lieutenant Ted Findlay."

"Good meeting you, Sergeant," Findlay said as he rose from his seat in a chair beside Bloodworth's desk. Besides the gray hair worn cropped close to his temples, Scully noticed the stranger's hollow eyes and gaunt, sunken cheeks. It was the face of a sick man, Scully thought. Scully also noticed that Findlay didn't smile, but just twitched his thin, bloodless lips a little in the manner of a man who is afraid to let his feelings show. His handshake was firm and brisk, though, and his greeting seemed genuine enough.

Bloodworth asked Scully to take a seat as Findlay sat down again, then he began telling Scully the reason for the meeting.

"These are aerial recon photos taken of a trestle bridge that the Japs have been using to transport supplies to their forces in the jungle," Bloodworth explained, spreading a group of glossy though somewhat grainy black-and-white prints out on his desk. "We obtained the Intelligence pertaining to the bridge partly as a result of the captured Japanese military maps that Sergeant Scully brought back from his patrol."

B-Company's commander went on to say that once the bridge was recognized to be an important conduit of supplies for enemy forces in the sector, it had become the target of sustained bombing missions. The long-range, high-altitude B-29 Superfortress bombers based in newly liberated Guam had flown into the area and destroyed the bridge superstructure using the new and sophisticated bomb sights that permitted extraordinarily accurate targeting of enemy installations.

"But even as the Superforts turned around and headed back to their bases, the Japanese were engaged in furious rebuilding activity," Findlay spoke up.

"This *one* particular bridge is very important to the enemy," he continued. "It's their link to the northern territory of the island, straddling a major supply line.

"To us, on the other hand, it's just as vital to shut down this route. We know that if we can kayo that bridge, then the Japanese resupply effort to their troops in the jungle will be seriously deterred.''

Scully wanted to know why the heavy-duty block-busters the Superforts were capable of dropping on their targets were not sufficient to accomplish total destruction of the bridge without benefit of additional assistance. Findlay, again running with the ball, explained to the sergeant that the important structural aspect of the bridge lay not in the trestle itself but instead in the gigantic concrete buttresses supporting it.

Lieutenant Bloodworth restated things for Scully's benefit. ''Those buttresses enable the Jap to throw up enough bridge to get their trucks over within only a few days' time, and not even the Superforts pack enough wallop to deliver the put-away punch we need to get the job done.

''That's where Findlay comes in,'' he continued after tamping down his pipe and lighting up the bowl. ''Findlay's an assault engineer, a demo man. The brass hats have sent him in to blow those buttresses sky-high. Sergeant, I want you and your platoon to see to it that Findlay gets to that bridge and does his job.''

Bloodworth added that Findlay understood he was to defer to the NCO's authority on all matters not relating to his direct duties. Findlay's business was blowing the bridge. Scully's was getting him there.

''Yes, sir,'' Scully answered, ''I understand, sir.'' He was already thinking about what this detail would entail. As usual, the job sounded dirty, but in this case it maybe sounded a little more so than usual. But it was no use griping about it, Scully realized. He didn't like the feel of it, but his was not to reason why. His job was to do or die.

"Findlay here will brief you on the rest of the details," Bloodworth went on to say by way of dismissal. "Draw whatever gear you need from stores. That's all, men." Saluting Bloodworth, Scully and the demo man walked out of the lieutenant's orderly room.

THIRD PLATOON was briefed by Scully and Findlay on the requirements of the job. Findlay fielded the questions put to him by the men in a precise, professional manner, but seemed cool and aloof. The men found him to be overly tight-lipped and downright unfriendly. Even for an officer, Findlay was not the sort of man they could feel at ease with.

Scully didn't like this fact more than anything else about the job that he and his troops had been called upon to perform. If his men were to find themselves going into a dangerous situation, then it was best that they did so without any undue morale problems.

Scully saw the potential for a big morale problem right away, considering Findlay's distant manner. But orders were orders, and Scully and his unit had no choice except to carry them out in the most soldierly manner possible.

After they had drawn supplies and packed their gear, the platoon boarded a six-wheeled transport

truck heading deeper north, into the interior of Luzon. The purpose of their trip was to link up with a
second man who was to accompany the unit on the
mission in addition to Findlay.

The other newcomer, according to the demo man,
was to be their Filipino guide. Scully was informed
that the Philippines native had been a member of the
elite Filipino Scouts and had survived the infamous
Bataan Death March, one of the few of the principals
who could boast of such a singular accomplishment.
The guide's village was a couple of miles distant and
lay on the path of their line of march toward the sector where the trestle bridge was located.

The transport truck rolled through roads that were
shattered and cratered from stray shell rounds dropped
by both sides in the fierce struggle to take the sector
away from the Japanese.

Scattered along the margins of the road and in the
deep ditches and fields of cane on both sides lay the
bullet-riddled, fire-scorched remains of mechanized
warfare that had been immobilized by pitched fighting to secure the sector.

The men of Third Platoon were as hardened as any
combatant to the grisly sights scarring the landscape
in the aftermath of battle. Every GI soon learned that
the only way to save his sanity was to look upon the
horror of war with a sardonic wit that took everything—even death—in stride.

Despite the evidence of fierce and bloody fighting
all around them, the dogfaces on board the transport

soon turned to conversation and cracking jokes. Those were familiar antidotes to the long periods of boredom, punctuated by moments of extreme panic, that were the infantryman's lot.

Eightball was in the process of winding up the story about the Italian foot soldier who was invited to Berlin to meet the Führer. "So he turned to Hitler and says, 'My Führer, my brave comrades and I will defend Rome to the last drop of German blood.'"

Hit with the punch line, the GIs broke into peals of laughter. Scully cracked open a pack of Old Gold plain ends and lit one up with his Army lighter, offering a smoke to Findlay. The demo man shook his head, then took out an old briar pipe from a pocket of his field jacket and lit up.

McGurk, Applebaum and Jacek engaged in a game of cards. The lowest bet was a thousand bucks with the pot going to one, then the other, until every one of the dogfaces became a millionaire at least once.

The sky was overcast when the transport truck lumbered up the steeply graded dirt road and came to a juddering halt inside a village of thatched huts, some of which were roofed over with tin sheeting. In this village of crude shanties the narrow streets were filled with children dressed primarily in rags.

Both children and adults regarded the GIs who rolled in on the heavy truck with sullen eyes, saying nothing, just giving the newcomers the native version of what the GIs had come to know as "the thousand-yard stare."

It was the stare born of hardship and soul-numbing oppression. Any GI who had seen serious combat time had worn it on his face at one time or another. So did the civilians who found themselves caught in the deadly crossfire of contending troops and war machinery.

Scully climbed down out of the truck and started asking in pidgin Spanish—the closest he could come to Filipino—for the guide they had come to meet, but his inquiries were hardly necessary. Scully looked down to discover that one of the urchins was tugging at his trouser leg.

"This way, senor," said the small boy to the American. With Findlay at the lead, the platoon followed a path until the child stopped before a dwelling. Through a doorway hung with beads, they entered into a dim interior smelling of cooking fish and frying grease.

Inside the shack was a small, wiry Filipino wearing tire-tread huaraches, loose-fitting trousers in the native style and a soiled athletic shirt. He sat on a bamboo platform honing a long, sharp knife called a barong, usually carried in an ornately carved scabbard worn at the belt.

"I am called Lafcadio," he said to the Americans, extending his hand to Scully. Standing, he held up the gleamingly polished, wicked-looking knife. Then, plucking a straight black hair from his head and effortlessly slitting it down the middle across the finely honed edge of the barong, he added, "And I am at your service."

18

Lafcadio had his gear packed and ready to go. All that remained for the unit was the final order from the patrol leader to move out. With Scully nowhere in sight, the troops of Third Platoon began wandering around the village. With time on their hands until the order came, and not yet knowing precisely when they would be scheduled to depart, the dogfaces followed their noses and their eyes.

From one of the shanties the enticing odors of spicy native cooking wafted out at the newcomers. A couple of GIs drifted over to check it out as though drawn by invisible fingers. They were welcomed by a well-rounded woman who was dressed in a sarong. At another hut they came upon an old man with a long, grizzled beard and skin as thin as ancient parchment. The old man was strumming chords and picking out notes on a guitar, accompanying himself as he sang native folk songs in Filipino dialect.

Scully had been weighing the pros and cons, and finally he decided that the platoon would not move out of the village until just before daybreak of the following morning. Dusk would be falling in a couple of hours. The men were weary from the day's march and would be more alert and combat capable if they left the village first thing in the morning.

A determining factor in the decision was Lafcadio's need to brief the American servicemen on what they should expect when penetrating the semimountainous jungle sector and his own need to be brought up-to-date by Findlay and Scully.

Maps of the area of operations were soon spread out on the worn-out cane furniture in Lafcadio's dwelling, with Scully, Findlay and Lafcadio taking turns in concisely outlining terrain features, enemy troop concentrations and movements, as well as the actual mechanics of blowing the bridge, buttresses and all.

Lafcadio's young son, Raoul, watched the goings-on with a great deal of curiosity. His big, dark eyes shone brightly, and his face, though dirty with brown smudges from the chocolate that had been handed him by the GIs, displayed the eagerness and the concentration of an intelligent mind.

Throughout the village other Filipino children were lining up to receive handouts from the American soldiers. Eightball, Finelli, Applebaum, Pee Wee, Jacek and the other members of Third Platoon went through the motions of a familiar ritual as they broke open their ration kits and doled out chocolate, candy and food items to the native children, whose outstretched hands, thin and sticklike from malnourishment, and hopeful bright eyes reached out to them imploringly.

If any of the GIs had any doubts about why they were fighting this war, the scene would have removed every last trace of it from their minds.

The war came home to a GI in many ways and made it personal. One of the ways that it got personal was on the battlefield. Another way was at such times as these, when the war's civilian casualties came face-to-face with the American foot soldier.

As the soldiers of the Los Angeles guard doled out their gifts, they saw not only grime and malnourishment but the unhealed scars of war, as well. Some of the children were missing an eye or an ear, others bore the burn marks from high-explosive on their thin arms. Still others walked with noticeable limps or bore ugly wounds that were barely concealed by the pathetic rags in which they were clothed.

Before the GIs was the most damning indictment of all on the Japanese drive to take the islands of the South Pacific. If a picture was worth a thousand words, then this one was the ultimate portrait of the price paid by innocents for territorial conquest.

As the jungle twilight thickened to the somber darkness of night, pierced by the shrieks of parrots and the hoots of monkeys from the branches of the high rain-forest trees, the GIs set up sleeping bags and bivouacked for the night.

Papajohn and McGurk were to stand the first watch, Applebaum and Finelli the second watch. Inside the hut belonging to the Filipino guide, Scully and the demo man made final preparations for the long, rough haul that lay ahead of them.

By the time Finelli was on sentry duty, the little village was quiet, wrapped in the healing arms of sleep. He settled in for a quiet spell, when suddenly he heard something rustle in the underbrush. Finelli raised his M-1 rifle toward the rustling noise and curled his finger around the carbine's trigger. It had to be the enemy. His throat tightened in anticipation.

"Okay, sport," he called out. "Show yourself," he went on, covering the bushes with the rifle.

"At ease, soldier," a voice said back to him, gruff and familiar. Finelli saw with relief that it was Scully. The sergeant was in full battle dress, carrying his Thompson SMG, this time outfitted with a drum magazine full of .45-caliber rounds. "I couldn't sleep for love or money. Thought I'd spell one of you lookouts."

"Thanks, Sarge. I can use the sack time. If you wanna know the truth, it's kinda spooky out here. I been imagining the whole Jap army is hiding in the jungle out there."

Scully watched Finelli disappear in the direction of the village and began walking his perimeter. Smoking on perimeter patrol duty was strictly against the rules, so Scully kept an unlit Old Gold plain end jutting out of the corner of his mouth.

What were they doing back home in Los Angeles? he wondered as he sat down on a rock. What the hell time was it there, anyway? Were the dames still as pretty as he remembered them? Were the beers still as cold, the java still as hot and the fries that you got on the side with a double cheeseburger smothered in ketchup still as good as they used to be? And most of all, wondered Sergeant Matt Scully in the middle of nowhere, would he live long enough to find out?

Maybe, Scully answered himself. And then again, maybe not.

19

At 0400 hours Third Platoon left the Filipino village behind them. Lafcadio and Judo were in the lead, Scully brought up the rear, with Findlay somewhere in the middle. The rest of the platoon formed a strung-out line or proceeded along the column's flanks.

The scruffy urchins of the village had come out of their shacks and lined up to see the GIs off with solemn faces. Some of the men patted them on the head and wondered if the children ever slept.

Here they were, up before sunrise but no different in appearance than they had been the night before—their somber eyes looking out of gaunt faces without blinking. The GIs looked back to see them waving, their hollow eyes still projecting the familiar thousand-yard stare.

Alone among the unit, Findlay paid no attention to this sad display.

The demolitions expert kept his face turned toward the jungle. His cold gray eyes were somewhere else. Not on the jungle itself. Somewhere else, maybe inside his head. But not the jungle, not the village, not anywhere that other men could understand.

SIX YEARS BEFORE, Findlay had been a third-year chemistry student at the University of Berlin. That was in the spring of 1939, just before Hitler's Nazis had invaded Poland. His family had money, and his education at the prestigious university was part of the family's plan so he could see Europe before returning to the States to begin his career at the family-owned chemical corporation.

From his apartment overlooking the Kurfurstendamm in Berlin, Findlay had witnessed the constant drama of the Nazi pageantry unfolding before his eyes.

More than once, Findlay had attended Nazi Party rallies at the Nuremburg complex. As an American he was awed and shocked by what he saw. Findlay understood that something far-reaching was taking place—something that would leave its mark on the world. He became obsessed with the unfolding threat and wondered why the rest of the world had let it go on for as long as it did.

Findlay realized that they didn't see the full extent of the danger—not Roosevelt, not Daladier and certainly not Chamberlain and his "Peace with Honour" group in Britain. None except for Winston Churchill, to whom nobody listened. Findlay's interest burgeoned into a full-blown obsession.

A few days after his graduation and his scheduled return to San Francisco, Findlay knew that Hitler would lead a procession through the streets of Berlin. From off-the-shelf chemicals, Findlay had assembled a crude but serviceable bomb. His plan was to carry it with him and throw it into the Führer's car when it passed.

Ranks of wildly cheering Nazis lined the streets. Standing among them in the front ranks was Findlay. He clutched the bomb he had made in sweaty hands, wondering if this was really an insane dream and if he would awaken at any moment to find himself in bed.

It was no dream, however. Minutes later Hitler's staff car drove up. As if on cue the crowd went wild, thrusting out their arms in the Nazi salute and crying out to their Führer with the same insane mass roar of mindless adulation that Findlay had already witnessed.

Then he saw Hitler.

The Nazi Führer looked directly at him. For a fleeting moment their eyes locked, and Findlay stared into the cold, soulless eyes of the Führer.

How long he stood there afterward, still mesmerized, Findlay didn't know. But when he came to his senses again, the critical moment was long gone. The procession of Nazi officials had passed him by. The bomb was still in the pocket of the oversize greatcoat that he wore.

Dejected, Findlay walked back to his flat and drank himself into a stupor. Two days later he awoke to find that his hair had turned completely gray. Soon after, he returned to America, aged beyond his years and having undergone a complete personality change.

Never forgiving himself for his cowardice, he determined that he would join the service. He saw action in Europe and elsewhere, destroying several bridges and performing railway demolition duty with the OSS. He had contracted malaria but never complained about his recurrent bouts. Though he made valuable contributions to the Allied war effort, Findlay had never forgiven himself for his moment of weakness in Berlin. Each mission he undertook was another penance paid.

LAFCADIO LED THE UNIT through a beaten path that snaked through the jungle. It was one of several old plantation tracks he was familiar with. According to him, the area through which they were passing was one of moderate though ongoing Japanese activity. They were spread throughout the sector, and the platoon needed to exercise extreme caution to avoid being sighted by the enemy. A confrontation was not on their agenda. Their mission called for covert penetration, not engagement, and the latter had the potential to deter them from the vital mission.

After a steady but stealthy march, Lafcadio led the troops to a spot where he said they could rest. Nearby a mountain stream ran with clear, cold water from which they could refill their canteens. He assured them that they could drink the water without adding the GI-issue purification tablets that killed bacteria and fungi but made the water taste foul and unpalatable.

Falling out against boulders and the trunks of coconut palms and other trees, the platoon took its rest break. They fished out tins of K-rations, and the troops filled their empty stomachs with much-appreciated Army grub while they rested their tired dogs.

Scully called Papajohn over and volunteered him for canteen-filling duty. Papajohn went around collecting the patrol's canteens, and Lafcadio pointed him in the direction of the stream, which meandered at the bottom of a gentle slope in the hilly, jungle-covered terrain.

Papajohn trudged down the slope and saw the stream a couple of minutes later. It was fairly large, strewn with boulders and running swiftly across them. Papajohn wondered if there were any fish in the stream and was sorry that he hadn't asked the Filipino about the possibility of catching any.

Looking cautiously around to make sure there wasn't any enemy activity, Papajohn squatted down at the edge of the stream and began filling canteens. He had filled a couple of canteens and added the purification tablets to each—no matter what anybody told him, he had no intention of drinking untreated water—and screwed down the caps, when a blur of movement on the other side of the stream caught his eye.

He froze in place while his heart pumped furiously and adrenaline set all his nerves on edge, making his muscles tense. A moment later he heard the sound of voices.

Then he saw the first Japanese soldier.

The soldier was walking up to one of the mangrove trees that grew beside the stream. He pulled down his fly, and then there came a familiar sound of a stream of liquid splattering against leaves. His companion joined him, saying something to the first soldier, then he moved away a little, pulled down his pants and squatted down.

Papajohn's knees and calves were already beginning to ache, but he forced himself to remain motionless in place. The enemy was close enough to easily see and hear him if he made any false moves. If there were others in the vicinity and any fire was traded, it could jeopardize the whole mission.

Remaining stock-still and stone-silent, Papajohn watched as the soldier stepped away from the tree and crossed to the edge of the stream. The other one finished his own business and joined his partner, and they busied themselves filling their canteens from the flowing waters. One of them stood up, but the other, having replaced his canteen on his belt, stooped to drink from the stream and wash his face.

Suddenly he lifted his head and seemed to stare directly at Papajohn across the width of the stream. Papajohn knew then that the enemy had seen him, maybe not even made visual contact, but seen him with his mind's eye with the instincts of a combat veteran.

The man straightened suddenly and stared hard across the stream, in the manner of a man who is not certain that he had seen what his intellect tells him is there. It looked for a moment as though the game was up as the Japanese soldier unfastened his holster and moved to cross the stream, beginning to slide iron from leather.

But unexpectedly, his companion called out impatiently. After shouting something back, the suspicious soldier cast a last look across the stream, then reluctantly walked away when his buddy called out to him again and waved him on with brisk gestures of his arm. Then both men faded into the jungle. Papajohn waited a while longer, then moved forward in a crouch. Finally, hugging the canteens to his body, he quickly made his way back toward the platoon's encampment.

20

When Papajohn finished his breathless account, Scully looked highly skeptical. "So you think there's a chance that one of the Japs might have seen you, huh?" he said more to himself than the private as he absently rubbed the stubble of his angular chin.

"Yeah, that's right, Sarge," Papajohn answered impatiently. He didn't much appreciate the sergeant's not taking his account seriously. He had two eyes in his head, and he knew what he saw when he saw it. "I could swear one of them spotted me. The other one called him away before he could do anything, though. If not for that, it might have been curtains."

"Okay, Papajohn," Scully said at last.

Scully turned and beckoned to several men. He wanted to put together a reconnaissance squad whose task was to sweep the surrounding area and locate the Japanese force Papajohn had sighted. "Jacek, Applebaum. You're coming with me and Papajohn. Mockler, you're in charge here while we're gone. Anything not in GI-issue gets it between the eyes."

"Check, Sarge," returned the corporal, making a gun with thumb and index finger and jiggling his thumb.

"I want to come, too," another voice put in. Scully looked up, surprised to hear Findlay volunteer for high-hazard duty. The demolitions man hadn't exactly struck him as being the action type.

"Nix on that, Findlay," Scully returned immediately. As far as he was concerned, Findlay was half a civilian, with a rank that was primarily symbolic. Despite his noteworthy intentions, he could only get in the way. "You're too valuable to the unit," he concluded. "You stay put right here and keep your head down."

Scully checked the ammunition clip of his tommy gun and made sure the pistol that rode in the pit holster across his chest was loaded with .45-caliber slugs.

From his gear stocks he removed extra grenades and suspended them from the iron gimlets studding the canvas webbing across his chest. The other members of the recon squad also made their preparations for battle, although a firefight was the last thing any of them wanted. An exchange with the enemy would only have the effect of alerting hostile patrols in the area that the opposition had been sighted, and it could potentially abort their mission in its initial stages.

Moving slowly and cautiously with Scully in the lead, the recon squad proceeded through the jungle toward the edge of the stream. When they reached the bank, Scully took the point and scoped out the area with seasoned eyes. The sergeant easily found the place where Papajohn had knelt to fill the canteen and then proceeded to recon the opposite bank of the stream.

Not noticing anything amiss, Scully used hand signals to indicate to the other members of the squad that they were to ford the stream. Scully went first, having already picked out his cover on the opposite bank. When he had safely reached it, he gave the sign to Papajohn. Before long all three members of the recon squad had crossed the stream in turn and succeeded in reaching its opposite bank.

Cradling their weapons to facilitate quick deployment, the recon unit moved into the underbrush lining the opposite bank and penetrated the jungle, pressing forward silently, using hand signals to communicate with one another and speaking only as a last resort and then only in a whisper.

They proceeded for some ten minutes through the dense brush to one side of a narrow, beaten path, avoiding the path itself, and soon came to a small clearing that was illuminated by pale shafts of sunlight filtering down through the rustling canopy of intertwining fronds.

There, in the clearing, they found the Japanese whom Papajohn had spotted at the stream earlier on. Scully counted six foot soldiers, all privates from their uniform insignia, except for a sergeant, who appeared to be somewhat older than the other men. Scully couldn't tell at first glance whether the troops were a detachment from a larger unit deployed farther in the jungle's interior, a scout patrol or simply the remnants of a larger unit that had been decimated in the recent fighting.

If Scully had to be forced to bet on it, though, he would have chosen the last possibility. The men appeared dirty and unshaven. Their uniforms were soiled and ripped. They had the raunchy, motley, battle-worn look about them that was characteristic of stragglers, deserters and those who had been on the losing end of a battle a few times too many.

The way Scully sized them up, the group functioned as a roving patrol. Possibly they would have orders to hit the enemy then disappear, the same hit-and-run pattern that seemed to prevail with the other enemy activity encountered so far on Luzon.

Papajohn sidled up to Scully, moving with catlike stillness on the jungle floor.

"What do we do about these Japs, Sarge?" he asked Scully in a barely audible whisper. "I say we pick 'em off right now. A couple of shots, and they're off to meet honorable ancestors."

"No," Scully replied just as quietly. "We got orders to escort the demo man to that bridge. Shooting's to be avoided if we can help it."

Then again, Scully didn't like the body language of one of the Japs whom they were spying on. He was gesticulating with his arms as he spoke with the sergeant, pointing in the direction of the stream. Scully got the distinct feeling that the private was trying to convince his sergeant about his sighting of an American.

"Is that one of the Japs you saw before?" Scully asked the private.

"I don't know, Sarge," he replied, scratching his jaw. "It's kind of hard to tell."

Scully thought for a moment as he continued to watch intently. He noticed that a second Japanese private had been called over by the sergeant, as if being asked to confirm what the first one was relating.

"Okay, just keep your shirt on until I tell you," he told Papajohn. "In fact, pass it on. I don't want anybody getting itchy trigger fingers."

Papajohn nodded and crept from Scully's position.

A couple of feet from where Papajohn had been standing, a trip wire made from twisted jungle vines and concealed in the brush was stretched tautly across the surface of the jungle floor.

One end of the trip wire was connected to a balance piece made from a section of felled tree. The other end was connected to a small bamboo peg hammered into the ground. Held in perfect suspension by this arrangement and hidden amid the rustling leaves overhead was a much larger stake carved from another log.

Papajohn didn't spot anything on the jungle floor as he moved along. Then he stumbled, and the trip wire pulled taut, activating the booby trap. He heard something slice the air overhead with a whistle that only a large object makes. Looking up, he saw a blur of motion from above. In the split second that he had left to live, Papajohn thought it was a snake launching itself through space to strike him. A moment later the stake impaled him right through the chest. The sharp tip penetrated his sternum, driving deep into lungs and spleen, then jutting out of his lower back, dripping with his blood.

Papajohn's tortured scream echoed through the jungle.

Scully couldn't stop to help Papajohn. The GI was beyond any help, and Scully had to look out for the rest of his men. Hefting his loaded and cocked tommy, Scully charged into the clearing, letting the chattering submachine gun roar and rattle in his vibrating fists. The Japanese unit reacted with catlike quickness, drawing weapons as they dodged for any available cover. One of the privates wasn't nearly fast enough on his feet to evade the hail of .45-caliber manshredders ejected from Scully's fire-belching Thompson SMG.

While he was scrabbling for his holstered pistol, he was lashed across the side by a brace of glowing, steel-jacketed rivets. The hydrostatic shock effect of sudden energy transfer from bullets to tissue caused his upper arm and chest region to explode in a shower of bright red blood. He was hurled to the ground in a half cartwheel that culminated with his booted legs kicking up in the air and his face shoved hard against the ground.

In the echoing seconds following the Thompson's stuttering battle cry, Jacek charged in right behind Scully, his Garand .30 blasting, adding its own distinct death rattle to the banshee chorus of Scully's ratcheting gun. By then, the surviving enemy had gone to ground and were returning fire of their own. Scully hollered for each GI to pick his man, and they engaged in a frantic stand-up gunfight, with the enemy forces trading fire without benefit of cover. When the firing ceased, all the Japanese were dead, and Jacek had caught a bullet in the fleshy part of the leg.

Applebaum dressed Jacek's bullet wound, and the squad searched the bodies for important papers. They found nothing except for the odd war souvenir and assorted personal effects. Scully gave a cursory glance to the contents of the prone sergeant's wallet and flung the photos, folded rice-paper letters and other possessions back onto the corpse. When the clearing yielded nothing further of seeming importance, and no evidence of other Japanese was found, Scully gave orders to his troops.

"Applebaum, head back to the rest of the unit and bring them back here on the double," he told the dogface. "The fire we traded with those Japs might have been heard by their buddies in the jungle, and it might not be too healthy for us to stick around here."

Scully asked Jacek how he was holding up, and Jacek flashed him the thumb's-up in answer. He reported that he could walk, which made things somewhat easier since having to rig up and carry him on a stretcher would have slowed them down significantly. Scully next faced the disagreeable task of collecting Papajohn's effects.

Impaled on the pointed stake of the booby trap, the dead GI was hanging limply, his head thrown back and the muscles of his face constricted in his final terror and agony. A pool of dark blood had collected on the ground beneath him. More was dripping slowly from the two points where the stake penetrated, then exited, his body.

Scully stripped the dead man of his dog tags and personal effects. He pocketed both in his field jacket and then together with Jacek pulled Papajohn off the stake.

"Leave him to me, Sarge," Jacek said softly, ignoring the pain in his leg. The sergeant nodded and turned away to scout the perimeter as Jacek got his entrenching tool out of his pack and began digging in the sodden jungle earth.

21

The platoon hurriedly pulled out, anxious to put distance between them and the scene of their brief but bloody encounter with the Japanese patrol. Jacek walked with a pronounced limp, but otherwise he managed to keep up his end of things. Although his wound was causing considerable pain, he put up with it silently, not uttering a single word of complaint.

As patrol leader, Scully demanded a fast and unrelenting pace from his men. The firefight had put him on full alert, ready for the possibility that the Japanese patrol had been in the forefront of a larger unit. If that was the case, when the patrol failed to report back on time, the whole unit could move out and close in for the kill.

Findlay was starting to have problems of his own. His malaria was making a comeback. Excitement or stress could bring on an attack, and even though he kept taking quinine tablets, the treatment didn't seem to be holding his symptoms in check.

A couple of the GIs in the platoon had noticed his shivering and sweating, and saw the jaundiced cast of his skin. When they questioned him about it, though, Findlay had curtly replied that it was nothing and told them in no uncertain terms that it was none of their business.

But Findlay was getting worse. He had trouble focusing, and his muscles were on fire. As waves of weakness washed over him, his knees sagged, and each step was getting harder to take than the one before.

Findlay tried to summon up the strength to continue on. The fever would pass, he told himself. The pain, too, would pass. Keep moving, just keep moving and don't think about it, he told himself. When he stopped for breath, though, he couldn't keep himself from tottering.

Scully turned as one of his men came up from behind. He also saw Eightball waving frantically from his position at the rear of the platoon.

"It's the demo guy, Sarge. Something's the matter with him."

Scully called a halt and walked back down the trail to find Findlay lying on the mossy ground among a grove of bamboo trees. His face was flushed and red and glazed with an oily coating of sweat, and his bloodshot eyes were rolling around in his head. His body was still shaking with chills. Scully had seen it before. Jungle fever. *Malaria.*

"How long have you had this, Findlay?" Scully rasped at the sick man lying on the ground. He suddenly remembered his first impressions of Findlay in Bloodworth's orderly room. "You were sick when you bought in to this operation, weren't you?"

"I figured I'd be okay," Findlay managed to answer hoarsely, speaking with much difficulty. "I *will* be okay. I just need a little water. Get me some water, will you?"

"What you need is a freakin' hospital, Findlay," Scully told him angrily. "And the rest of us Joes need our heads examined for being such prize chumps."

Scully turned and stalked away, muttering curses to himself. He sat himself down on a rock and watched Lafcadio and other members of the unit sit Findlay up, give him a drink and dab some water from their canteens on his forehead.

Having a sick man along complicated matters. Jacek was bad enough with his wounded leg, but Findlay was far worse a problem for the unit. They needed to make tracks in a hurry, or they could well end up being wiped out by the Japanese army.

Scully contemplated the option of sending Findlay back to the company command post with Finelli and maybe another guy to ride shotgun. He couldn't really spare any man, but the way things were looking, that might be the best thing he could do.

Findlay, though, had other ideas. After a couple of minutes he succeeded in standing shakily, swaying to and fro but nevertheless shrugging off Judo and Lafcadio, who tried to help him.

"I'm okay now, Scully," he said. "I can make it."

"*Sure* you can make it," Scully grunted. "About two feet. Maybe less." He shook his head in disgust.

"I can make it," the demo man insisted. "Trust me, Scully."

"Findlay, you're a liability to this unit," Scully answered him in a growl. "You had no damned business signing on in the kind of condition you're in. The lives of every man in this outfit are now in danger because you loused up. So I'm gonna put it to a vote. All for going on, sound off."

"I'm for going on," Eightball put in. "If Findlay says he can do it, then let him show us what he's made of." Applebaum, Finelli, McGurk and the rest of the detail added their own affirmations to the vote of confidence.

Scully called Lafcadio over and asked the Filipino approximately how far away from their objective the platoon's present position put them. Lafcadio paused a moment and considered. He then informed Scully that in his opinion they were no more than a day's march to the bridge site. Considering the wounded and the sick men, though, they might have to allow for another day of travel to be on the safe side.

"Okay, Findlay," Scully intoned after the Filipino had spoken. "Looks like you win. But listen to me and listen good. If you drop and can't go on, I can't spare a man to take you back. We leave you where you lie with as much rations and water as we can spare, then you're on your own. If you can accept that, then we're continuing. If not, I'll send you and Jacek back to camp right now."

"I'm in, Sergeant," Findlay insisted without a moment's worth of hesitation.

"Okay, then," Scully concluded with a nod of his head. "Let's not waste any more time jawin'. We got us a job to do. Let's go do it."

LIEUTENANT NAKASHIMU received the secure radio transmission sent by his forces in the jungle. The report on his desk detailed the outcome of a confrontation between a scout detail and what was surmised to be a force of the enemy who had come to take the Philippines from the Imperial Japanese Army.

Nakashimu paced his office and looked out through the window. He could see the brown-green mountains in the distance, the sun beating down like a blazing ingot in the clear sky. The lieutenant was a shrewd man and one who had the gift of putting together the pieces of a puzzle.

He believed that he now saw a connection between the repeated attempts to bomb the bridge into rubble and the presence of an enemy contingent deep in the jungle. The bombing attempts had failed, and the Americans were at a loss as to how to proceed. It was only a matter of time, he had surmised long before, before they attempted to accomplish the job by some other method.

Nakashimu gave immediate orders for patrol activity to be stepped up. He wanted to make certain that the bridge remained intact because there was an important convoy scheduled to pass over it before long.

Nakashimu did not want anything to hinder the convoy in reaching its objective.

CONTINUING THEIR MARCH through the jungle in the oppressive heat, Scully's unit came to a place where the jungle foliage grew somewhat less thickly. Nearby was an abandoned village, according to Lafcadio. The Japanese had pressed most of the villagers into slave labor to repair the trestle bridge farther inland, as well as work on other fortifications that were in need of maintenance.

After posting sentries, Scully gave the men a much-welcomed opportunity to rest, smoke a few butts and sit around eating their field rations. Although Scully wouldn't have bet a plugged nickel on it earlier, Findlay seemed to be holding his own and had even managed to keep up a respectable pace, although from time to time he had to be helped by other members of the unit.

Jacek's leg wound, on the other hand, was getting worse. The sulfa powder wasn't doing much to encourage the healing of the wound. In the humid tropical climate even the smallest cut could fester in no time at all. The wounded private was having a hard time walking but tried his best not to show it. It was too early to call so far, but Scully saw discouraging signs.

A couple of GIs had no stomach for food and after a few bites were feeling restless. They decided to take a look around the ghost town. There wasn't much to meet the eye, though. The abandoned village was completely desolate, and it looked as if the enemy had scavenged it clean.

In the humid, uncomfortable heat of the night, sleep didn't come easily. They lay awake restlessly turning and tossing, seeking some comfort for aching bodies. Every shadow seemed alive with the enemy, bristling with guns and vibrant with unknown danger. The night was as dark around them as their future.

22

The platoon had ventured onto land that was climbing steadily. The relatively flat coastal plain gave rise to often steep hills farther inland. Dirt roads hacked out of the jungle wilderness switchbacked between the densely foliaged hillsides.

The pace of the small combat unit's trek became more strenuous due to the natural obstacles inhibiting the progress of the foot soldier. Scully was soon finding it necessary to schedule more-frequent rest breaks, and the men were grumbling more and more as time passed.

"Isn't there a better way to get there?" Scully asked Lafcadio at one point, realizing that the men were being pushed to their limits. The wiry Filipino shook his head and shrugged his shoulders in answer.

"No," he replied finally. "The land is rough and wild here. Your men will just have to get used to the pace of the march." Soon they would reach their destination, he assured them. The men would have to learn patience. Their bodies would accommodate them before long, after having adjusted to the rigors of the trek. They would just have to push on as best they could until then.

Scully glanced up at the burning tropical sun. The higher altitudes of the more mountainous terrain did nothing to alleviate the humidity and omnipresent stench of moist earth and rotting vegetation of the dense rain forest. The men of the platoon marched along their route with their sleeves rolled up, their field jackets stripped off and tied around their packs, their helmets perched high on their sweat-drenched fore-heads.

Findlay lagged behind the rest of the group again. He had been making better and better progress, but the altitude and stress of the climb had brought on another malarial attack.

Findlay realized that this was happening when he became aware that he was beginning to hallucinate. Suddenly he saw a water buffalo galloping down the hillside. Head lowered, horns out, it was charging straight for him. Findlay could see its nostrils flare as it snorted angrily and he heard the drumming of its hooves. Shaking his head to clear it made no differ-ence. He could see what he saw as big and as real as life.

"Move aside! Get out of the way!" Findlay bel-lowed, cowering behind some boulders. "Can't you see it! Can't any of you see it coming?"

Eightball and Applebaum were running at the cow-ering demo man in two seconds flat. Reaching him first, Applebaum clamped his hand over Findlay's mouth to stop him from yelling again.

The sound of his scream had echoed off the surrounding hills. To the members of the unit it seemed as though it might well be heard all the way to Tokyo.

"Shut up, Findlay!" Applebaum hissed through clenched teeth in the sick man's ear. "You're gonna bring every damned Jap from here to Borneo down on our asses."

Findlay made moaning sounds in response. He'd been seeing things, he realized. He signaled that he was all right and tried to free himself.

"You promise to keep it buttoned up if I let you go?" Applebaum asked. Findlay shook his head assertively. Applebaum looked up at Scully. At a nod from the sergeant, he eased off his grip. Helped by Applebaum and Mockler, Findlay regained his feet, no longer seeing things that weren't there.

But Findlay was not the only problem Scully had to contend with. No sooner had the march resumed, when Pee Wee Drummond came running up to Scully from his position on the flanks of the patrol unit.

"Sarge, it's Jacek," he told Scully. Drummond acted as the corpsman of the unit because he had finished a year of premed before enlisting. He had been tending to both Findlay and the wounded Jacek for some time. "His leg's in really bad shape. Sarge, I don't think he can walk anymore."

"Rig up a stretcher," Scully ordered Pee Wee, who grabbed Barrows and pressed him into service. Fortunately there was enough loose bamboo lying around

on the ground so that the materials necessary to fashion one were readily available.

Using two long pieces of bamboo for support, they
lashed smaller crosspieces between them with jungle
vines and lay Jacek on top of the makeshift but quite
serviceable stretcher. The men were assigned to take
turns carrying Jacek. The march resumed once more,
although even slower by this time, hobbled with the
injured man who was running a high fever and was
delirious.

"Annabell, don't give him the time!" he moaned in
his fever-warped fantasy. "Annabell, you're *my* girl.
You hear that, Annabell! One day you're gonna be the
mother of my children!"

"What's he jabberin' about?" McGurk asked
Drummond as they picked up the stretcher when it was
their turn. "Who's this Annabell?"

"Annabell's his girl back home," Pee Wee answered. "Jacek's got real problems," he continued
sagely, shaking his head. "Gangrene in the leg and a
dame on the mind."

"Well, I wish he'd shut up," McGurk returned to
Drummond. "He's giving me a case of the heebie-
jeebies with all that freak talk."

"He don't know what he's saying," Pee Wee told
McGurk. "Don't pay him no attention."

"I don't care what you say," McGurk shot back.
"Jacek's giving me the creeps, I tell ya."

At the next rest break in a small clearing, Scully
went over to Jacek's stretcher and knelt beside the

private. Scully wasn't a doctor but he didn't need a medical degree to be able to tell at a glance that the GI was in a bad way.

His wounded leg, bandaged with a bloody rag in the absence of fresh dressings, was giving off a foul odor from the gangrene that was eating it away. His eyes were rolling around in his head, his face was ashen gray and his entire body was covered by a thick, oily fever sweat.

"He as bad as he looks?" Scully asked Pee Wee, who stood nearby.

"Worse, Sarge," Drummond responded. "If that leg won't come off pretty soon, he won't make it. The gangrene's getting worse every minute."

That decided it for Scully. He called the Filipino guide over and put a question to him that he didn't really want to ask but was now forced to by circumstances.

"Lafcadio, we need medical attention for Jacek," he began. "You know anyplace in this hill country where we can find us a doctor?"

The unit's guide didn't even have to think for a moment. "No doctor anywhere nearby," he stated with certainty, shaking his head. "But there is a priest, a Father Benigno, who treats the sick around here."

Lafcadio pointed in the direction of the sun. "His church is a half day's march over that way."

Scully considered the information he had just received and weighed the possibilities. The detour to the church could well cost them days. On the other hand, there was no way of continuing on with one severely wounded man and one very sick one, both of them delirious with fever.

In the end Scully felt that he had no choice but to detour toward the church in the hopes of finding help. Having made up his mind, he issued orders for the unit to detour toward the church of Father Benigno.

23

Judo and Lafcadio went ahead to reconnoiter the area. Although the church was just where Lafcadio had remembered it, it appeared to be deserted.

The well-tended herb gardens and copra groves were overgrown with parched brown *kunai* grass. The building itself looked to be in a state of complete disrepair, damaged by shell strikes and its masonry rotting from lack of maintenance in the jungle heat and humidity.

Entering the confines of the church, the two scouts found themselves suddenly confronted by a figure wielding an ancient double-barreled shotgun. The figure had jumped out of the shadows, and Judo at once moved to fire his Garand at the attacker.

"No!" Lafcadio shouted, jumping with desperate speed in between the two men, his hands raised in a gesture of supplication. "Do not shoot! Do not fire at him!"

"I know you," said the figure a moment after Lafcadio had yelled out, stepping from the shadows and lowering the shotgun. "You are Lafcadio the blacksmith and maker of knives, are you not?"

In the sunlight filtering in from outside the church, both Judo and Lafcadio could now see clearly that the man with the shotgun wore the turned-up collar of a Catholic priest.

"Yes, Father," Lafcadio said in answer, crossing himself. "It is true. I have come here with American soldiers. One is very badly wounded and needs immediate care."

The padre shook his head in dismay, and a sigh escaped his lips. "This terrible war. How it has ravaged this country. It was poor before, but there was joy also at times. Now there is only sorrow."

He turned to Judo. "Look at me, American. I am a priest, yet I greet those seeking solace in this house of God at the point of a rifle, fully prepared to shoot them dead. What will be the end of all this evil and madness?"

"I don't like this war any better than you do, Padre," Judo told the priest. "But the Japs started it, not us. We're the ones who are gonna finish it."

"Finish it! When is the slaughter of war truly ever finished?" the padre mused out loud. "Still, I hope it is the American side that wins. The Japanese, they are barbarians. They know no mercy."

Father Benigno wasted no more time in talk. He invited the troops to come into the church; indeed, he hurried them inside as quickly as possible. The Japanese were in the area, he knew full well. Some had been by the church as recently as the day before yesterday. Jacek and Findlay were brought into the parish house beside the church building, where Father Benigno looked them both over with a critical eye.

"The wounded man is in a very bad way," he told Scully, who, along with Pee Wee and Judo, stood over the stretcher-borne Jacek. "The leg will have to come off. The sick one," he added, looking toward Findlay, "more quinine and some rest. Maybe it will pass. Maybe no. Only time will tell."

"Can you do anything for the man with the wound?" asked Scully.

"Yes," the padre answered. "I think so. But I must begin right away. Boil water," he said to Lafcadio. "I will need it to sterilize my instruments."

"Annabell, Annabell!" Jacek cried out. "Don't listen to him, Annabell!" Father Benigno shook his head and made the sign of the cross. These times were truly hard and men were sorely tested by them.

LIEUTENANT NAKASHIMU watched as with the respect due to his rank the private presented himself before him. "Honorable Lieutenant," he said when he straightened up again. "We have found proof that the Americans were in the vicinity."

The private held up scraps of torn khaki fabric.

The lieutenant stared at the scraps, noting what appeared to be the presence of blood, and then took his sector map from its case. Here was evidence that one of the men might be wounded. Yet the group of Americans might have gone anywhere. The forest was vast and had many hiding places.

Consulting his map, Lieutenant Nakashimu saw that a church was located nearby. He did not know

whether or not anyone still tended the place or if there
was a congregation left among the populace. Still, it
was a likely choice for men to take refuge in, especially with casualties in tow. Speaking quickly and
shrilly and gesturing with his hands, Nakashimu gave
orders to march at once toward the church.

"I HAVE GIVEN him a sedative to help him sleep," Father Benigno said to Scully. It was many hours after he
had begun the amputation operation. Now he was
bone-tired from the exertion he had undergone.

Assisted by Pee Wee and Lafcadio, he had removed
the soldier's gangrenous leg at a point just below the
knee and saw to his relief that the gangrene infection
had not yet penetrated deeply enough to affect the
bone marrow.

"I think I have successfully isolated the infection.
Your private should be all right," he told Scully in the
large room above the altar where the men of the unit
sat and waited.

Scully wondered if Jacek would feel the same way
about it as the priest when he finally woke up from the
ether he'd been given. He might live or he might not,
but one thing was for sure—Jacek wouldn't be doing
much dancing anymore at the ballrooms he had fre-
quented back in Los Angeles.

Scully lighted up a smoke and offered the padre one.
Father Benigno accepted the American cigarette
gratefully and sucked the fragrant smoke deep into his
lungs. "Ahh," he said, relishing the taste of the to-

bacco. "It is a long time since I have enjoyed a good cigarette. Our country grows the finest tobacco in all the world, but now..." His voice trailed off as he inhaled again.

"Not much left after the Jap got through with it, huh?" Scully finished the sentence for Benigno, already anticipating a familiar complaint about the rapacious enemy.

"This church was founded two hundred years ago," the padre said when he next spoke. "It has survived famine, floods, earthquakes, all the many hardships that the Lord visits on the land and men alike. Yet until the Japanese came, there were services on Sunday and baptisms several times a year, and the land was peaceful and things grew in profusion. Now all is in ruins and disarray, and I am alone here in this empty house with no flock to lead."

Scully didn't know how to answer, but was saved the trouble by the sudden appearance of Smitty Hargett, who had been posted as lookout in the belfry.

"Trouble comin', Sarge."

"Spell it out."

"Jap column," Hargett answered, spitting out a brown gob of cut plug tobacco. "I saw them clear as you please from the bell tower. They're heading straight for the church."

"Okay, padre," Scully told the priest. "You better get yourself into a safe place pronto. Lead might just start to fly pretty soon."

Father Benigno abruptly stood up, and his eyes burned like living coals. "No!" he shouted. "This is a house of the Lord! I decide what happens here. There will be no shooting in this house. Not just because I am opposed to violence, but because the Japanese will surely take revenge on this church and certainly burn it to the ground in retaliation for any damage done to them."

Then the padre told Scully what he wanted done instead. The old priest instructed Scully to pull his troops together and to hide them in the root cellar of the church.

Father Benigno promised that he would get rid of the Japanese. Scully saw it best for them to accede to the padre's wishes. After all, he and his men were the ones seeking refuge in the padre's church. Besides, they were not in a good position to fight, and a showdown with an unknown force could certainly stop them dead in their tracks, far short of accomplishing their important objective. Reluctantly Scully and his troops climbed through a trapdoor in the sacristy beside the altar and down a flight of steps that led into the basement of the church. Soon they heard the sound of campaign-booted Japanese marching into the building while they hunkered down in the darkness.

24

"We have reason to believe that American troops are in this vicinity," said the Japanese lieutenant. "If you know of their whereabouts, tell us now and we will leave you in peace."

"I know nothing, honorable sir," Benigno returned, his face expressionless. "I am all alone here."

"You have heard nothing of Americans, then?" the lieutenant pressed, his coal-black eyes searching the priest's face and probing his gaze.

"Nothing whatsoever," Benigno answered, not lowering his eyes but instead continuing to stare fixedly into the lieutenant's hard and arrogant gaze.

"You will not mind then if my men have a look around?" asked Nakashimu.

"How could I raise any objection," Father Benigno observed, "when your men are already freely looking everywhere without permission even having been asked."

The remark earned the padre a rap across the face from the lieutenant. The emperor's chosen leaders of a new order in the Pacific did not require any man's permission to do as they wished.

"Insolent dog!" Nakashimu shouted at the padre, and slapped him again, even harder than before.

"Think well before replying flippantly to a soldier of the Imperial Army. Be warned—next time I will shoot you for giving such an answer."

Lieutenant Nakashimu then stomped around the church, looking around with eyes that missed nothing and took in every detail. Some fifteen feet below the hobnail-studded soles of Nakashimu's campaign boots, Scully's platoon looked up at the creaking ceiling above their heads.

The dogfaces could clearly hear the enemy soldiers marching around above them. Muted sounds of men bellowing orders, punctuated by the dull, heavy thud of furniture being shuffled around, echoed through their hiding place.

The GIs followed the course of the activity up above, turning their heads in reaction to every fresh thud as the soldiers ransacked the place in their fevered search for the American soldiers.

Sweat broke out on the faces of the concealed Americans, and their fingers tightened on the triggers of their weapons reflexively. Not a man among the khaki-clad servicemen could say for sure that he wasn't claustrophobic as they waited together in the dank storeroom constructed to keep wine, cheese and other edibles against the tropical heat.

"Sarge, shouldn't we hit 'em now?" McGurk asked, afraid that he was no longer able to stand the tension. "What if the Japs find us down here? They could, you know. We'll be trapped like rats with no way out."

"Button your lip, McGurk," Scully said back in a whisper that rasped like a hacksaw biting into a length of pipe. "Do as you're told, and everything comes up roses. That goes double for the rest of you eight balls. Any man who thinks he's better off shooting at those Japs will have to deal with me personally."

Having put the fear of God—of an entirely different sort than Father Benigno's brand of religion—into his men, Scully settled down and waited as tensely as the rest of the unit.

Up above them, the Japanese lieutenant probed everywhere but succeeded in detecting nothing. His men fared no better.

"We have found no sign of the Americans," Sergeant Kondo reported to his superior with a bow after he had conferred with the rest of his men.

The lieutenant threw up his hands in frustration and turned to take his leave. There was no point in prolonging their stay. The church was a dead end. Probably, he considered, the Americans had never come here at all. Perhaps they were still somewhere in the accursed jungle.

"Go!" Nakashimu hollered at his men. "We are finished here."

At that precise moment, Jacek cried out below in the cellar.

"Annabell, oh Annabell!" he shouted. "Not with that greaseball, you don't! He'll give you the clap for sure!"

Hearing the muffled cry, the departing enemy soldiers stopped dead in their tracks. Looking up at the ceiling, Scully and his platoon could hear raised voices and thudding of boots. It was apparent to all of them that the Japanese had stopped because they had heard Jacek cry out.

"What was *that?*" shouted Nakashimu at Father Benigno. The priest stared at the officer, his mouth agape and unable to utter a single word. Down in the wine cellar Scully put his troops on alert, readying them for battle. It looked as though they would have no choice except to fight it out. Fortunately the resourceful Filipino guide had another idea. Urgently he asked the GIs to hold their fire and asked to be given a chance to try the ploy he had in mind.

Drawing his gun and flanked by two of his men who ported their rifles, the lieutenant stalked toward the front of the chapel. There was a sacristy located on one side of the altar. Inside it was the trapdoor that led down to the cellar where the American troops were hidden.

Nakashimu pushed into the confines of the musty-smelling room. Two brisk strides and he was inside. He saw someone or something move in the shadows. Nakashimu slid his pistol from his side holster and pointed it at the sudden flicker of motion in the darkened room.

"You there. Come out! Show yourself or I'll shoot!"

Lafcadio stepped from the shadowed recesses of the sacristy. The Filipino had his hands high up in the air. "Please don't shoot!" he cried out as he drew closer.

"Search the room!" Nakashimu shouted at his men, who shouldered past the Filipino and proceeded to tear apart every corner of the sacristy. "You, come here!" Nakashimu next barked at Lafcadio, gesturing with the barrel of his pistol and eyeing Lafcadio and the room around him. In moments, the muzzle of his pistol was pointed at the Filipino guide's head.

"Don't shoot, honorable sir!" Lafcadio pleaded again. The officer stared hard into his face. Had he thought to look down at the Filipino's bare feet, he might have found the prize that he was after all along, because Lafcadio was standing directly atop the trapdoor leading to the staircase.

"Who are you?" Lieutenant Nakashimu demanded in a loud, hectoring voice. "Why are you hiding here?"

Before Lafcadio could utter a single word in response, Father Benigno appeared beside them. He had managed to storm past the soldiers in the nave area of the church. He did not know what was going on nor understand what was happening. He only prayed that the Lord would give him the strength and the luck to carry him through the next few tense minutes.

"This man is my servant," he shouted at the lieutenant when he saw Lafcadio and grasped instantly what was happening. "He is harmless, as I'm certain you can see. Lower your gun. There's no need for the weapon."

Just then the lieutenant's men reported the results of their search. They had been unable to find anyone else either inside the sacristy or outside of it.

"Why didn't you tell me about this servant of yours?" Nakashimu asked, somewhat mollified. "What else are you hiding from me, priest?"

"Nothing, *nothing,* I quite assure you," Father Benigno answered with his hands outstretched in a gesture that was a plea for understanding. "Fondido here is a little slow in the head," he went on, making a circle with his forefinger at one temple. "He is really like a child. I was afraid for him, afraid that he would be terrified and do something rash. Sometimes he even soils his bed, you know. That is why I told him to run and hide in here when you came. Is that not so, Fondido?"

"*Sí*, it is so," Lafcadio answered, attempting to sound like a simpleton. "The padre, he tell me 'Fondido run, Fondido hide, the boogey man, he is coming for you, Fondido.'"

Lieutenant Nakashimu gave a grunt of distaste and looked hard at Lafcadio one more time, as if to probe his mind and sift for any trace of guile or artifice, then looked hard at the priest in turn.

"Very well, then," he said finally. With a set of shrilly barked orders, he commanded his troops to leave the church. Below, in their hiding place, Scully's troops heard the staccato crack of the enemy's boots as the contingent marched out. At a nod from Scully, Eightball took his hand from Jacek's mouth and Mockler let go of his legs, which he had been holding to keep them from kicking out.

When the enemy was finally gone, Father Benigno rapped three long, three short, on the trapdoor, giving the all-clear signal to the Americans. Scully was the first out of the cellar, and he sent Eightball and Hargett running to the windows to see if any Japanese were still around. Shortly they came back, reporting that there were none to be seen.

"You think we fooled them, Padre?" Scully asked.

The priest shrugged. "All I know is that they are gone," he told the American sergeant, anger apparent in his voice and demeanor. "And I hope the same goes for you Americans very soon. This war has brought enough misery to this troubled house."

25

When Jacek regained consciousness, he asked for water. Pee Wee Drummond brought him some from his canteen. He lay on a canvas cot provided by Father Benigno and asked how long he'd been out. Nobody told him about his leg yet. Nobody had the heart.

"Two days you been out," Drummond answered.

Then Jacek remembered his wounded leg. Suddenly he felt its painful throbbing beneath the sheet covering the lower half of his body.

"Jeez," he cursed. "Just got the worst cramp in my leg."

Pee Wee didn't say anything in response. He continued to stare at the other GI.

Jacek reached under the blanket and felt for his leg. His fingers closed around empty space. For a moment his eyes went wide with horror in his face. He had to be hallucinating again, he figured. A second ago he'd felt the intense stab of pain in his leg. Now the leg wasn't there anymore.

Finally he summoned the courage to pull back the blanket. When he did, he looked and saw that his left leg was gone at the knee. He stared hard at the stump swathed in bandages and finally began to cry.

"God almighty!" he wailed. "Why my leg? It should've been someplace else. But not my leg! Not my fuckin' leg!"

"At least you're alive," Pee Wee told him lamely.

"But don't ya see, I can't dance no more," Jacek returned, realizing with a sharp pang that he would never be able to make movies like his idols Gene Kelly and Fred Astaire, that he would never go to Hollywood and make his dream come true. "And if I can't dance, I might as well be dead."

"Hey, don't talk like that. You got no right to after what we went through to get you here," Drummond retorted angrily.

"How am I gonna keep up with you guys?" Jacek asked sulkily.

"What do you mean?"

"We're movin' out, ain't we?" Jacek asked. "With this bum leg, I'll never be able to keep up."

"That's easy. You won't come with us. Sarge's orders," Drummond went on to explain. "It's all fixed up with the padre. You're staying until either we come back to get you or the Japs get kicked out of the area."

Jacek didn't have an answer to what he'd just been told by the private. He just sat there and sulked some more at this latest piece of news. It was all too much to digest at once. He had to get his bearings. Everything had changed for him. His life, he realized, would never be the same again, even if he did make it back home alive. "Leave me alone, will ya," he said finally. "Just leave me to myself."

Father Benigno was standing outside the door of the room in which the wounded man lay. He had heard everything that had gone on inside and felt deeply for the troubled young man who had journeyed so far to suffer so greatly.

"I will talk to him," he told Drummond. "Perhaps through the Lord's grace he will come to understand his situation and make peace with himself." Saying that, the old priest went into the room and prepared himself to help a soul in torment.

Elsewhere in the church, Scully and his troopers of Third Platoon were getting their gear ready. At first light they would be marching out of the area and getting back on the track toward their original objective, the trestle bridge that Findlay was to dynamite out of existence in order to cut the enemy supply line on Luzon.

"How'd he take it?" Scully asked Drummond when he joined the rest of the unit in the church's refectory, where they were billeted during their stay.

"He didn't like it," the private responded. "He didn't have much choice, either."

"It's all for the best," Scully commented. Turning to Findlay, he said, "I feel like I should order you left behind, too. You're a heap of big trouble, fella. That malaria you got could act up again, and the closer we get to the Japs, the more danger that puts us in."

"I'll be okay," Findlay protested. He held out his hands for Scully's inspection. "See, Sergeant. Not a tremor. Solid as a rock. Thanks to a little rest and some quinine, I'm as good as new."

"For now, sure," Scully replied. "As far as the long haul goes, let's just say I have my doubts. But you're the linchpin of this operation, Findlay. So I guess you come with us after all."

From somewhere off in another part of the church building, they could suddenly hear Jacek crying out in anger and despair and the sound of Father Benigno praying for the salvation of his soul.

TWILIGHT'S FIRST GLEAMING saw Third Platoon marching away from the church in a jungle-covered landscape that was shrouded by the dense mists of a pea soup fog and interspersed with a steady drizzle of tepid water.

The fog collected in the hollow places of the land and formed an impenetrable curtain. The rain did not refresh, but only turned the ground to mud that sucked at the soles of the infantrymen's boots and contributed to the hothouse humidity of the jungle.

The men had the sensation of being lost in a timeless, spaceless wilderness where the environment played tricks with sound and distance. The cries of parrots and squirrel monkeys in the trees above punctuated the fog as the men marched through it, as if to mock their passage through their ancient realm.

Before long, as the sun rose to its zenith, the fog burned off and the oppressive heat of the day began to settle down like an invisible burden that they had to carry on their shoulders along with the rest of their gear. Though it was slightly cooler because of the somewhat higher altitudes, the heat and humidity were stifling. The men marched bare chested, wearing only their helmets for protection, although these too were stiflingly hot under the steady beating of the near-equatorial sun.

As their Filipino guide had predicted, the men had become fully acclimatized to the stresses of the difficult trek and no longer needed frequent rest breaks. Even Findlay seemed to have no problems keeping up with the rest of the troop now. The demo man was alert, and though he still took quinine pills against the microbes that lived in his body, he seemed to be free of fever and sickness.

A little more than a day after they had set out from the church, they were informed by the Filipino guide that they were in the general vicinity of the bridge, within only a few miles of it cross-country. Depending on how fast their progress was and other factors, such as weather and terrain, the platoon could expect to reach the bridge before noon the following day.

Although the bridge itself was not yet visible, Lafcadio pointed out various terrain features that he knew lay in close proximity to the bridge itself. These were visible from the top of a particular hill in the mountainous country where the platoon took a much-needed rest break after long hours of steady climbing through unpredictable terrain and dense vegetation.

From that vantage point Scully could discern a network of switchbacking jungle roads following the unpredictable contours of the land. Lafcadio explained the need for special precautions and vigilance because the Japanese were heavily entrenched in the area.

As if in proof of that assertion, Scully suddenly saw a transport truck rounding a turn in the snaking roadway and proceed due west before disappearing around another bend. The truck bore the icon of the blood-red sun emblazoned on its dun-colored flanks. It was a Japanese transport.

Refreshed and rested now, the members of the unit shouldered their gear and continued the trek, descending into a densely jungle-covered area. When they emerged from the region, they would be in the immediate vicinity of the bridge.

With Judo and the Filipino taking the point, the platoon proceeded along a beaten track that Lafcadio knew about, a track the Filipino claimed would bring them close to their destination. None of the members of the platoon noticed that among the dense foliage and stands of large-leafed vegetation flanking the trail, there could be discerned the telltale outlines of Japanese helmets.

Lieutenant Nakashimu had not believed the old priest of the church for a moment. He had not been born a fool. Even as the priest told him his lies, Nakashimu could sense that the Americans were somewhere close at hand, possibly within the church itself. However, he was a wise man and did not wish to risk exposing his men to the possibility of a trap, nor himself for that matter.

If the Americans were indeed sequestered within the church, then there was sure to be bloodshed. A better way was to confine the bloodshed to the enemy's ranks. Nakashimu had sworn to die for the glory of the Nipponese Imperial Empire and for his Honorable Emperor Hirohito. Slaughter without reason did not conform well to Bushido, the warrior's code of honor in battle.

Let the slaughter be confined to the ranks of the hated round-eyed enemy, Nakashimu decided. They could wait to deal with the old priest for his treachery later. The lieutenant and his troops waited patiently in the bushes for their victims to enter the killzone. With his *Shin Gunto* raised and ready to strike, Nakashimu prepared to deliver a mortal blow that would elevate him to eternal glory and damn the Americans to eternal hell.

26

"You know where I wish I was right now?" Applebaum asked Barrows.

"Alaska," the GI replied without hesitation.

Applebaum was getting ready to say that he wanted to be in Sam's Diner just off Santa Monica Boulevard, having a cup of java and a slice of fresh-baked apple pie smothered in butter pecan ice cream, but the unexpected answer caught him off guard.

"Whaddaya mean Alaska?" he asked.

"I mean Alaska as in cold," Barrows said without a moment's pause for reflection. "In case you haven't noticed, Bud, it's plenty hot where we are right now."

"Yeah, I guess I never thought of it that way," Applebaum had to admit.

"Plus, with Alaska, you got the Eskimos," Barrows went on glibly.

"So what?"

"So where you got Eskimos, you got igloos. And I'd give half my demobilization pay to climb right inside an igloo right now."

"Yeah, I suppose you got a point there," Applebaum returned. Sam's Diner had seemed a good idea at first, but Applebaum could see Barrows's point about Alaska and the igloos of the Eskimos. It made a lot of sense.

All he could think of was how darned good it would feel to climb inside one of those igloos. In one hand he'd have himself an ice-cold Coke. In the other one, he'd have a fifty-cent Havana cigar. Now that's what he called the berries.

"You know, Barrows," Applebaum began, but suddenly stopped as somebody hit him in the back with a rifle butt and he staggered forward, heavy-footed and rubber-legged. He began to ask, "Hey, who's the wise guy," but the next moment he realized that a red geyser of hot blood was pouring from the hole in his ruptured stomach.

For Rudy Applebaum the supreme moment of truth had arrived. Every single question Applebaum had always asked himself about how he'd take it if he ever caught the proverbial bullet with his name on it was answered in a split instant of blinding revelation.

The answer was nothing at all. It was ridiculously simple. He was pitched forward by a force that he had no power to resist, and he dived into the black, bottomless pit suddenly yawning up at him. Applebaum hit the ground and lay still in the embrace of death, the beginnings of a smile on his face, a smile that would have appeared enigmatic to anyone except Applebaum himself.

Violent firing had broken out all over the place. Scully realized that the platoon had walked straight into an ambush. The underbrush was alive with Japanese wearing snippets of leaves, and branches festooning their helmets and uniforms for camouflage.

The Japanese were everywhere, shooting with a vengeance and making raw-steel bayonet charges with the banzai war cry on their peeled-back lips. The world was like a seething cauldron of fire and steel around them, resounding with the fury of battle and the groans of the wounded.

Caught off balance, the platoon fought back with desperate speed, taking cover behind fallen trees and boulders, and in hollows.

McGurk was crouching behind a tree when a stick grenade came bouncing his way. He jumped to one side, keeping the soles of his combat boots turned toward the grenade's splinter radius. His ears rang from the blast as the stick grenade detonated a scant moment later.

Stunned and disoriented, McGurk scrambled to his feet but realized he'd lost his gun in the process of diving out of harm's way. Then he saw the Japanese soldier charging toward him. He seemed to come in slow motion, laughing and grimacing as he raised his rifle to shoulder level and charged with his bayonet pointed right at McGurk's throat.

Stunned by the grenade blast as he was, McGurk scrabbled for the .45 holstered at his hip and tried to shoot. But before he could get his service pistol clear of its leather case, he was struck in the chest with the sharply honed cutting edge of the rifle bayonet.

Pulling out the blood-glazed weapon, the enemy prepared to strike again. At last McGurk succeeded in clearing the .45 from its leather sheath. He cocked the hammer and squeezed off a round.

Caved in by the force of the heavy-caliber ACP slug entering at point-blank range, the Asian face disintegrated in a hot red gush of blood. Still, the Japanese soldier kept on coming. Even with most of his head gone, the adrenaline-charged body retained its momentum for a second longer.

But the steam had been taken out of the banzai charge. The man's legs collapsed under him as though made of straw, and he tumbled to the ground, his body twitching and jerking. McGurk finished him off with a salvo of .45-caliber rounds until the body stilled forever.

Barrows had caught enemy steel in the first burst but had managed to set up the .30-caliber machine gun on its legs. With a tourniquet applied to his wounded shoulder and his teeth gritted against the searing pain, the Third Platoon squad gunner let the ambushers have it.

"Eat lead, Tojo!" he shouted as he whipsawed the machine gun on its tripod mount to unleash blazing automatic fire at the charging Japanese.

It was an incredible sight to behold. The Japanese seemed gripped by some unseen hand, as though they were being propelled forward. Their ferocious battle cry filled the air. "Aiieeeeyahhhh!" It sounded like a long, shrill, drawn-out syllable that brought his blood temperature to a chill.

Their eyes wide, their teeth bared with determination, the emperor's soldiers charged directly into the stream of whirlwinding automatic fire.

Even though the hailstorm of rotoring .30-caliber lead chopped them down like straw men braving the hurricane, they kept coming on. There seemed no end to the suicidal, human-wave charge. It was as though they were eager to be cut down by the blazing heat of Barrows's chattering weapon.

Finally the Japanese stopped coming, having exhausted their ranks in the assault. Already attracting hordes of buzzing insects in the steaming tropical heat, their corpses littered the killing ground. Barrows finally untensed his finger from the machine gun's trigger.

"Sound off!" Scully shouted. There was no point to worries about giving away their positions. The enemy knew where they were and had stopped the assault for reasons that had nothing to do with stealth anymore.

Eightball sounded off, followed by Finelli, then McGurk, Barrows, Mockler and the rest of the squad, including Lafcadio. All except for Applebaum, Smitty Hargett and Findlay, the demolitions man. "Smitty, Findlay, sing out!" Scully shouted again.

"Forget about Smitty," Scully heard Judo yell back a few seconds later. "The Japs cleaned his clock."

Judo was squatting beside the disfigured corpse that had been torn practically limb from limb by jagged shrapnel from a hand grenade burst. From the looks of things, Judo figured that the potato masher must have gone off practically right on top of Smitty. He only hoped his good buddy hadn't seen it coming.

"What about Findlay?" Scully asked. "Anybody seen him?"

There was no answer. Findlay was lying motionless on the ground. He had been knocked unconscious by a rifle-swinging soldier who in turn had caught a fatal bullet from one of the GIs' weapons. But Findlay was beginning to come around. McGurk, closest man to his position, heard him groan as he came to. Creeping toward the demolitions man, McGurk assured himself that Findlay was still alive, although sporting a nasty bump on the head.

"I found Findlay, Sarge," McGurk's voice called out. "He got himself a bump on the head. Otherwise he looks all right."

"Don't let him out of your sight, McGurk," Scully instructed.

"Check, Sarge," McGurk replied.

A moment later the Japanese put up a white flag.

27

"American GI Joes!"

The voice shouted out from the Japanese lines that were strung out along the densely interlaced underbrush. A no-man's-land about twenty feet in width separated the Sunshine Division soldiers from the enemy.

"We are flying the flag of truce. We wish to confer with your ranking officer."

"Don't listen to him, Sarge!" Eightball cautioned Scully, crouching close at his side. "None of them can be trusted. He's trying to pull a fast one on us!"

"It is in your interest to reply!" the Japanese called out again, making another attempt to communicate with the Americans who were, like his own men, concealed by the dense matting of lush tropical vegetation and screened by the shadows of the dark rain forest. "Like yourselves, we are honorable men. Send out your ranking officer. We wish to speak with him."

"What you want to talk about, Tojo?" Scully shouted back across the small clearing, his voice instantly seeming muted, as though the very sound of his shout were absorbed by the dense growth and the humid darkness of the jungle environs.

"Who is talking?" came the retort.

"Sergeant Matt Scully. I'm the head man of this outfit. Say your piece—we don't have all day to sit around and powwow."

"I am Hasho Nakashimu. My rank is lieutenant," the officer called back from his position several feet away. Scully heard the rustling of leaves and saw signs of movement from where the voice came.

A moment later he was able to make out the form of a Japanese soldier rising from within a bamboo thicket. Beside him stood a private carrying a white rag tied to a bamboo stick. The private was waving the stick solemnly back and forth, as though he had an unpleasant task to perform yet had to do it anyway.

"Come out and talk," the enemy officer called out to Scully again.

"Talk about what?" Scully asked, cupping his hands before his mouth and shouting to be heard.

"You surrender, of course," Nakashimu answered him right back. "What are you afraid of? Come out. Surely you are not a coward, Sergeant."

Hearing the words, Scully's jaw set in a tight, grim line. He wasn't about to take any man calling him a coward, especially a Japanese, whose commanders had committed one of the most cowardly acts in the history of mankind when they sent out their Zeros to bomb Pearl Harbor.

Cowards? Scully thought. The Japanese had written the book on the subject practically. Following up their sneak attack on Pearl Harbor, they had swarmed across the dozens of islands in the Pacific, spreading death and destruction wherever they went.

Further proof, in Scully's mind, was the forced march of American and Filipino prisoners captured on Bataan through the jungles, killing most of them rather than risking the possibility of real men challenging them later on.

"Pass it on. Keep me covered," he told Eightball with a growl, smarting at the implied insult. "I'm going to talk to that Jap. Judo, you come with me."

Breaking from cover, Scully and Judo approached the small clearing between the two opposing factions. The Japanese lieutenant and the private who carried the white flag did likewise.

As the Americans approached the center of the neutral ground, they could make out the glittering eyes and raised weapons of the enemy squatting in the bushes behind the officer who was coming toward them with slow, deliberate steps, like a man who wanted to show all onlookers that nothing frightened him.

Scully stood face-to-face with the lieutenant moments later. He saw that Nakashimu was as tall as he was, with penetrating black eyes and a lean, almost triangular face. At his belt hung the *Shin Gunto,* the officer's samurai sword with the cord-wrapped hilt and specially forged blade with a lethal cutting edge.

Close up, Scully could sense that something was wrong. At least by American standards there was. The lieutenant had an aura of imminent danger and unpredictability. He was a man poised on the edge of violence, a man who would stab you in the back as soon as shake your hand.

Scully noticed that Nakashimu kept his hand near the holster hung on the Sam Browne belt he wore around his waist. Scully's own fingers were never far from grabbing distance of the .45-caliber pistol he wore on a military chest rig strapped across his heart. The familiar weight of the pistol there was reassuring, a powerful friend who could be called on in time of trouble.

"I'm here, Tojo," Scully growled at the lieutenant. "Speak your piece."

Nakashimu laughed. "I enjoy your colorful American witticisms, Sergeant," he told him in precise though accented English. "But to the point—your men are hopelessly outnumbered. You have no choice but to surrender. We will treat you according to the accepted conventions of war. Do not cause any further bloodshed. Issue the order to surrender now."

Scully laughed out loud at the lieutenant's nerve. The man had to be out of his mind if he thought that he had a snowball's chance in hell of getting the Americans to lay down their arms and surrender. It was just like the brazen-faced Japanese to want to do it the easy way, Scully thought.

"Sure, pal," he replied, looking contemptuously into Nakashimu's eyes. "You'll treat us according to the Geneva conventions. Just like you treated us at Pearl Harbor, Bataan, Corregidor, Guadalcanal and a dozen other places I could name. Sorry, but the answer's no soap radio.''

Nakashimu's face darkened as though a storm cloud had passed over it. He wasn't used to being addressed in such a manner, especially by a noncommissioned officer who did not even match him in rank.

Nakashimu was the scion of samurai, the offspring of a line of Japan's ruling elite that stretched back across untold generations to the days of the shoguns and well before even that. He knew that the Americans—whom he considered barbarians—had no understanding of such things, but all the same, he was still angered.

"Very well," he said curtly to Scully. As he spoke, he moved quickly yet surely and purposefully. From behind his back he pulled a concealed pistol, its barrel jammed between the thick leather belt and the rough cloth of his bush jacket.

Swinging the gun around, the officer made to put a bullet right between the insolent American's eyes. But Scully had been expecting trickery, and he was prepared for the sudden move on the lieutenant's part.

Whipping his left arm up the instant that the lieutenant made his play, Scully blocked his gun hand. At the same time, he unleathered his .45-caliber cannon in a beautifully coordinated movement of hand, wrist and arm, brought it up and fired off the weapon in one smooth, lethal motion.

Nakashimu's gun went off, but the shot was wild, high and on the outside. Scully, on the other hand, had his target behind the eight ball. Three ACP rounds in quick succession blew a gaping raw hole in the lieutenant's imploding abdomen, bowling him over with a rush of blood spurting up from his internal organs.

As the lieutenant went down, Judo took care of the flag-waving private with a series of lightning-fast kicks and jabs that splintered the man's gun hand and then the bones of his cheeks and jaw in rapid succession.

Concentrated autofire immediately erupted from the positions of Third Platoon and the Japanese. The steady rattle of the Browning was interspersed with the faster, higher-pitched ratcheting of the tommy guns, M-1s and BARs carried by the unit, and was answered by automatic fire from the Japanese shooters crouching in the bushes beyond the clearing. McGurk, Drummond and Eightball were scythed down instantly, victims of Japanese steel.

Scully and Judo were caught in the deadly crossfire as they snapped off bursts of lead, making their way back to their line by dashing forward, snapping off fire, then running forward again.

While they made their stop-and-go moves toward cover, Judo sustained a hit in the leg that sent him toppling to the ground. Still alive, but badly wounded, he gritted his teeth against the searing pain of his torn musculature and shattered bone.

Scully saw the private fall and started to go to drag him back, but a burst of autofire stitching the ground at his feet forced him to sprint the rest of the way back to his own men without Judo in tow. Gaining the last few feet between himself and the blazing guns of his men, he saw their hands reaching out toward him, heard their shouts encouraging him on to safety. Diving for cover, he landed hard on the fleshy part of his shoulder beside Eightball.

Scully realized now that the Japs could steamroll them without half trying. Not counting Judo and the also-wounded Barrows, Scully's unit had been whittled down to a mere handful: Findlay, Finelli, Mockler, the Filipino and himself.

There was no way on earth they could hold out against the Japanese force, which was most likely company strength, especially with the enemy capable of securing reinforcements from nearby bases.

"Sarge, you got to make a run for it," Barrows told him, as if reading Scully's mind. "Me and Judo will hold off the Japs long enough for you and the rest of the guys to get clear."

Scully indeed saw that Judo, though wounded, had managed to crawl to cover and was firing away with his Garand, snapping fresh rounds into the automatic weapon's receiver from the mag pouches that festooned his military webbing.

"It's suicide," Scully said to Barrows.

"It's the only way out, and you know it, Sarge," Barrows answered, trying to mask the fear he felt and knowing the grim prospects for his survival all too well. "We'd only slow you down. The Japs would end up getting us all, and after what happened to the officer you shot, they'd cut all our heads off and eat our brains for dessert."

As much as he hated to acknowledge it, Scully knew that Barrows was right. The Japanese wouldn't be taking any prisoners now. Not after the severe loss of face they had suffered by the killing of their officer— no matter that he had pulled the gun first and invited the payment he had received at Scully's hands.

"Okay, you win," Scully admitted. There was no denying it. Barrows's way was the only way now.

Quickly calling together the remaining men, Scully explained what was happening and instructed them to gather up all spare ammo and weapons. Two packs were loaded with them and thrown to Judo's position beyond their line, and the rest of the gear was left behind with Barrows. "God bless you, buddy," Scully said.

"Goodbye, Sarge," Barrows replied stonily, reaching around and pulling off his dog tags, then digging into his pockets to bring out his wallet and other personal effects. "My family's address is in there. See that they get this stuff, okay, Sarge?"

Scully took the personal effects with silent reverence. He had no more words left to speak, and the squad of those who would live to carry on the fight was already vanishing into the engulfing darkness of the jungle. Scully had to make tracks, too. He turned quickly, not trusting himself to say another word to the brave and tragically doomed man, and made for the rustling foliage that marked the passage of the GIs ahead of him.

Then they were off into the dense jungle brush. Soon, behind them they could hear the rattling of Barrows's Browning machine gun, punctuated by bursts of .30-caliber repeating fire from the Garand rifle ported by Judo.

They moved quickly away from the pitched fire-fight, and the sounds of battle soon receded to the fading din of distant conflict. Then there came the sounds of explosions—several of them booming in the distance in rapid succession. And then the firing abruptly ceased, and Scully knew that the guns of two of the bravest men that it had been his honor to know had been silenced forever.

28

The night was moonless when the Filipino guide led the tattered, battle-scarred remnants of Third Platoon to a patch of high ground overlooking the trestle bridge that they had come to destroy. From their vantage point, and through the still night air free of thermal distortion, the bridge was clearly visible to the naked eye, lying not more than three hundred yards from their position.

Findlay broke out field glasses and inspected the trestle bridge through lenses specially coated for night viewing. Satisfied that the aerial reconnaissance photographs on which he had based his preliminary assessment had been accurate and that he had chosen the correct method of blowing the bridge, Findlay handed the binoculars to Scully.

The sergeant then made some assessments of his own, based on his own military perspective. What he was looking for were signs of a beefed-up Japanese presence and increased activity around the bridge. Perimeter guards, extra sentries, anything that would indicate to him that the enemy had caught scent of the unit's mission and had set up obstacles to stop them.

A couple of minutes' worth of the close scrutiny convinced Scully that this was probably not the case.

There apparently wasn't any extra security at the bridge, none that was noticeable, at any rate.

Indeed, the strength of the entire guard detail appeared minimal. It consisted of two sentries who paced back and forth from one end of the bridge to the other. There was a guard post at one end of the bridge only, and it was manned by two other men.

It was amazingly low security for so vital an installation, but then again the Japanese could be notoriously unpredictable in their assessments of risk, and their lines did happen to be thinly stretched. For Scully the numbers added up. He decided that the situation warranted proceeding with the mission.

Scully knew what needed to be done under the present circumstances. Originally the plan had called for the platoon to secure the bridge. Next Findlay would place his TNT charges, and finally the charges would be detonated, blowing the buttresses clear out of the riverbed.

The situation had changed drastically, though. There were hardly enough men left in the unit to ensure that the bridge would be taken before one of the guards stationed in the guardhouse got off a radio SOS for reinforcements.

Scully decided that the objective could be realized with a slight alteration in tactics and a little bit of luck. He figured they had some of the latter coming to them at that point. The plan would stay basically as it was with one small change.

Instead of first securing the bridge in a lightning raid on the sentries, they would rig the bridge without alerting the Japanese. Then they would set off the demo charges, exploding the trestle, support buttresses and the guards in one big bang. After that they would do their level best to get away from the hellstorm at ground zero.

"Findlay," Scully asked in a whisper. "A couple of questions. One, can you rig the charges yourself, and two, how long will it take?"

Findlay scoped out the bridge through his binoculars one more time before answering Scully. "It's a one-man show, Sergeant," he said to Scully. "I think I can have it all wrapped up in a half hour to forty-five minutes."

"Then let's get to it," Scully said to the men. Issuing orders rapidly now that the operation was in progress, Scully stealthily led his troops toward the foot of the first of the three buttresses supporting the bridge and a point directly below the approach to the bridge. He could hear a radio droning in and out of hearing range from the guardhouse located directly above them. They were so close that he could smell the pungent odors wafting out of the guardhouse from a kettle of fish stew they were cooking up inside.

The booted feet of the two sentries walking their perimeters thudded atop the planking at the edges of the road surface in the center of the bridge. Scully could not only clearly and distinctly hear the sound of the two sets of campaign boots pass each other, but he could actually gauge the movements of the sentries on the bridge by glimpses through the chinks in the loosely placed planks on the walkways to either side of the road surface.

"Go," he said to Findlay, shoving him forward when the sound of the sentries' boot steps had receded into the night. Findlay clambered down the embankment and, reaching the first buttress, ascended the iron rungs set in its side for use by maintenance crews. He climbed to a few feet below the underside of the bridge and, suspending himself by using climbing tackle at the precise point required to produce maximum damage, he began working with practiced speed and skill.

Scully nudged Mockler. "You watch the guardhouse, Mockler. Get going."

"Check, Sarge," Mockler said, then he was scrambling up the earthen embankment with catlike quickness. Moments later the GI was in position, silently watching the sentries from the shadows, a thin smile on his face at the anticipation of paying the enemy back for Barrows, Judo and a whole lot of other good men.

"Finelli, get down to where Findlay's working. Keep your eye glued to him and those sentries up there."

"Gotcha, Sarge." Finelli wasted no time and hustled down toward the water's edge.

"Lafcadio, stay here with me," Scully told the Filipino guide. "Keep your eyes peeled for trouble."

Lafcadio was porting a tommy gun taken from one of the American KIAs and carried extra ammunition in magazine pouches at his belt in addition to the handmade barong knife. Grenades were also strung from netting draped around his chest. Scully knew he could count on the wiry Filipino in a scrap and was glad to have him thrown in with his unit.

Tensely they waited while Findlay got down to business.

29

Findlay was already working on the second buttress, directly beneath the center of the bridge. The TNT bundles he had carried with him in his pack were in place, nestled in the shadowy crotch where the underside of the bridge and the buttress converged. He had finished hooking them up to one of the three cables that would eventually be connected to leads on the plunger detonator destined to set off all three bundles of high explosive.

When that happened, the bridge would go sky-high, and with the trestle supports gone, the Japanese wouldn't be able to repair it any time soon.

Things ran like clockwork for a while. Then Findlay hit a serious snag when he fumbled and dropped a screwdriver he was using to tighten one of the lugs securing a bare wire lead to the second TNT bundle.

He cursed softly as the fallen screwdriver clattered on a rock below and hit the murky water of the sluggish river with a splash that seemed loud against the silence of the night.

He froze as though he had just been turned into a block of ice. Only a moment before, he had heard the rhythmic cadence of the sentries' campaign boots thudding on the planks of the walkway overhead.

Now the sound of the boots abruptly ceased as though the sentry had stopped in midstride.

A moment later Findlay heard the thudding of the footfalls on the creaking planks above him begin moving in his direction.

There was the clink of gunmetal against the railing of the bridge, and Findlay knew that the sentry was peering down over the edge into the darkness below. Not daring to move and thereby risk detection, Findlay mentally willed the shadows to close over him like an impenetrable shroud as he hung immobile, precariously perched above the razor's edge of destruction.

It was fortunate, Findlay judged, that he had been working where he was, his position not directly visible over the margin of the bridge. If the sentry was not persistent enough or thought that the sound he had heard was natural in origin and therefore innocent, then it might yet go all right for Findlay.

But a few moments after the first sentry craned his neck over the edge of the bridge, the second sentry's footsteps were heard as he loped toward the first man and joined him. For Findlay, it was beginning to look bad at that point.

"What was that sound?" the second sentry asked.

"I don't know," the first sentry responded as he continued to peer curiously and suspiciously over the edge of the bridge into the shadowed landscape of the defile below. "I thought at first it might be a jungle animal fishing for the river trout. But I have seen nothing."

The second sentry unhooked a flashlight from his belt. Holding the torch aloft, he shone its widening beam down into the defile, but the probing shaft of light revealed nothing but rocks, tropical vegetation and the sinuous and unceasing black expanse of the river flowing beneath the bridge.

"I see nothing, Yato," said the second sentry as he flicked off the flashlight and replaced it on his belt. "What do you think?"

The first sentry reflected for a moment. He was certain that he had heard something down there. Something that was not merely an animal scurrying on its way through the darkness.

"I'll climb down and have a look," he said.

Scully, Finelli, Mockler and Lafcadio had seen what had happened from their respective positions and were watching as carefully as night-hunting hawks. At first they hoped that the sentries would let the matter go once their initial efforts had failed to reveal a threat. But they saw that, true to their luck so far, the first sentry wasn't going to let matters rest.

From the angle of the sentry's descent, Scully and company could tell that he could not miss eventually catching sight of Findlay. And when that happened, it would be all over but the shouting.

The two Japanese stationed in the sentry booth were looking at the bridge sentries, too, although they didn't appear to act like men who were concerned that anything serious was happening. One kept stirring the soup kettle while the other dragged on a cigarette and watched the bridge, his rifle slung over his shoulder, occasionally calling out to ask for a rundown on the other sentry's progress.

In Scully's assessment, salvaging the mission from the latest setback demanded immediate action. It was a matter of now or never. Rapidly he hand-signaled to his men that they were to take out the two on the bridge and the others in the guardhouse, but take them out silently if possible. The squad deployed immediately, knowing that the more quickly they moved, the better their chances were of success.

Hearing the sentry scuttling down the side of the defile, Findlay drew his service revolver and silently cocked the trigger, ready to drill the sentry. One or two pulse beats later, Findlay saw the man's legs appear in the corner of the embankment that was visible from his position. He raised his Colt .45, but Finelli saved him the trouble of using it.

Finelli saw that the descending soldier would be screened from the other sentry's view for a few seconds by a hammock of earth when he set down at the bottom of the draw by the river's bank. Drawing his long combat dagger from its side scabbard, Finelli waited, tense and dangerous in the shadows, his entire body coiled to strike with deadly speed and power, ready to make every second count.

When Finelli made his move, the sentry never knew what hit him.

Finelli did it strictly by the book. Grabbing the man from behind, he muffled his mouth to prevent him from crying out. At the same time, he slid the knife between the sentry's short ribs, angling its razor-sharp tip upward and shoving it in hard to pierce the ventricles of the heart.

The terminated sentry in his arms writhed and flailed with berserk ferocity for a few seconds, and Finelli was afraid at one point that he couldn't hold on to the writhing body. Then suddenly, his last reserves of strength exhausted, the Japanese went limp as a wet rag, all the fight going out of him like water draining through a sieve. Finelli lowered the dead and suddenly very heavy man to the muddy earth, hearing the breath go out of him in a strange, dry rattle.

While Finelli was doing his part, Scully and Lafcadio had reached Mockler's position at the guardhouse. They could see the second bridge sentry leaning over the iron rail, sweeping his flashlight over the void and calling out into the darkness to his comrade.

The two Japanese in the guardhouse were beginning to realize that something was wrong. The one inside who had been stirring the stew pot put down his ladle, grabbed his rifle and came out to join his partner, who was already hefting his own gun. Both of them stared at the third man in the middle of the bridge, who gestured toward them, yelled something and turned to look down again into the shadows.

At that precise moment, Lafcadio and Scully moved almost simultaneously, each getting his man from behind. The Filipino used the long, wickedly sharp barong knife that he had pulled silently from its ornate scabbard in his belt. He thrust the dagger repeatedly into the sentry's back between his shoulder blades, holding him fast with amazing strength despite the dying man's fierce contortions.

Scully's own GI-issue dagger tasted blood, too, as he plunged it into the throat of the other sentry, propelling him through the open door of the guardhouse and sending him toppling against the pot of boiling fish stew.

The big cast-iron kettle was overturned and the already dead man went tumbling to the floor, the kettle crashing to the planking after him with a clang and a sickening hollow thud.

The last man on the bridge raised his rifle and prepared to use it. He was panicked to the bone by the sights and sounds of pure hell breaking out all around him. In his distracted state he didn't know whether to fire over the side of the bridge or at the hostile commandos who had appeared from out of nowhere by the sentry box.

While he was making up his mind, Finelli was running forward, waiting until the last moment to cut loose with a burst of the M-1 in his fists, having realized that there was no way to take out the fourth man silently.

Suddenly the panicked sentry fired his rifle, but his salvo missed Finelli. Finelli charged forward as the sentry fumbled with the rifle's bolt action and raised the weapon for another volley. Just as he fired, Finelli stumbled across a protruding nail head sticking out of the walkway and pitched jerkily forward. Landing on his face with the wind knocked out of him, he heard a bullet crash into the planks next to his head, a mere breath away.

Moving quickly, he managed to rise to a crouch, but this time the sentry got lucky, plugging him with a bullet right through the chest. As his lungs filled with hot, bubbling blood, Finelli cut loose with a .30-caliber broadside from his M-1 carbine, and got his man with whining hot lead, making his killer pay his dues before the Reaper claimed him.

Throwing up his arms, the sentry flew through the air before he collapsed in a twisted heap against the bridge railing, then the body tumbled over into the river below.

Scully was the first to reach Finelli where he lay sprawled on the planking of the bridge, bleeding his life out through the hole in his chest. "You'll be okay, kid," Scully said, cradling Finelli's head in his hands.

"You don't have to kid me, Sarge," Finelli replied, coughing up a crimson stream. "It's curtains for me. Just promise me one thing," he asked Scully, clutching at his field jacket with manic strength. "Please, Sarge, promise me."

"Anything, partner," Scully said back, staring into Finelli's imploring eyes, which were already getting that faraway look deep inside them. "You just name it."

"Promise me you'll write my mother and tell her I went to heaven." Finelli's hands clutched at Scully's collar. "Please, Sarge. Tell her that I went to heaven, not hell. Tell her that her son died like a hero. Promise me, Sarge."

"Yeah, partner, I promise you," Scully said to Finelli, his voice growing husky from the many conflicting emotions that churned around inside him. A moment later the hand that was grasping the collar of Scully's battle-grimed fatigue jacket with such superhuman strength slipped from the cloth and fell lifelessly to the planking, and Scully knew that Finelli had just been issued his pair of angel's wings.

"You think any Japs heard the shooting?" Mockler asked. He'd moved up behind Scully and heard Finelli's last request.

"Maybe, maybe not," Scully answered, not looking at Finelli anymore. "All the more reason to rig this baby and do what we came for." Suddenly he realized that he'd forgotten all about Findlay. Running to the edge of the railing, he called down. "Hey, demo man, how much longer?"

"A couple more minutes, Sergeant," Findlay shouted back. He had heard, though not seen, the furious action of the last savage minutes. "How'd it go with the Japs?"

"It was a regular riot. One of these days I'll write you a letter. Now hurry it up," Scully told him, and walked back toward the guardhouse. There he found Lafcadio looking through some paperwork, intently scanning the pages as he flipped them back and forth.

"Sarge," Lafcadio told Scully, "this is important."

Scully took a pocket flask full of Scotch out of his field jacket and unscrewed the cap. "Is it more important than this drink? If not, I don't want to know about it." He hoisted the flask in a toast to the bloody corpses of the dead Japanese lying nearby and took a slug.

"It is very important, Scully," Lafcadio said back earnestly. "These papers are duty lists and time schedules. According to them there will be an important supply convoy coming across at 0600 hours. That is not in very much more time, is it?"

Scully's expression changed as he screwed the cap back on and replaced the flask in his pocket. He regarded the Filipino with gimlet eyes, eyes full of suspicion, concern and a dozen other emotions. "You sure about this?" he asked the little guy. "I mean, really positive, Lafcadio?"

"Positive, Sergeant," the Filipino answered right away, thumping the documents in his hand with a forefinger. "These papers state what I have told you conclusively."

"Hell," Scully cursed out loud. The new development put a whole different varnish on things. Now there was no way he could blow the bridge yet, no way to walk away from what he understood to be his duty as a soldier and as an American.

Even if the convoy were delayed, he would have to chance putting a hold on the demolition job. Taking a Japanese convoy out with the bridge was worth the risk, and none of the men would say any different. Still, he'd have to put it to a vote. As matters now stood, and orders to the contrary, it was the only fair thing to do.

30

They were staying. The decision was unanimous.

Moving fast, Findlay rigged the final bundle of charges to the third buttress. Taking hold of both ends of a stick that he had inserted through the center hole in a cable spool, he strung the coil of demo wire from the foot of the bridge to the thickets surrounding the base of the high ground overlooking the trestle structure.

Once Findlay had paid out the length of demo wire, he went back over the path of the wire to its point of origin. Then he covered over the cable with leaves and mud to camouflage its presence.

While Findlay was doing his job, the rest of the team busied itself with hiding the evidence of the raid. Finelli was given a hero's burial on the riverbank nearby. The job had to be done hastily, but the squad knew that Finelli would understand and approve.

That left the Japanese KIAs.

The body of the dead sentry who had fallen over the side of the bridge had fortunately not drifted too far downstream and they were able to retrieve it. After stripping the body, they concealed it among the high, dense thickets of reeds and tall grass growing at the bank.

The other two bodies from the sentry box were hidden, too, but first they were also stripped of their uniforms. Trial and error proved that their uniforms fit Scully, Mockler and Lafcadio—not perfectly by any means, but good enough for what they had in mind, which was to create a diversion to stall the Japanese convoy that was expected very soon.

Lafcadio at first wanted to go it without one of the commandeered uniforms. He hated the Japanese so much that he initially declined Scully's urgings to put one on. Scully had to explain the situation to him twice before he finally relented and sullenly pulled on the enemy combat apparel.

The plan hatched by Scully was to occupy the guardhouse when the supply convoy arrived on the scene in a couple of hours. He went by the theory that the enemy would be suspicious if the bridge was unmanned upon their arrival. Their suspicions aroused, they might even stop short of crossing it. The Filipino was crucial to the plan's success, since he resembled a Japanese more closely than any of the others in the unit.

Masquerading as a sentry, Lafcadio's role was to signal the lead truck of the approaching convoy that the bridge was open and safe for them to cross. Then he was to sprint across it, as if meaning to get out of the way of the oncoming trucks that he had waved on.

Once Lafcadio reached the guardhouse, which was situated at the other side of the bridge, Findlay—who was stationed on the lip of the high ground overlooking the defile—would blow the TNT charges on the buttresses, sending as many of the trucks as possible into the defile below along with the destroyed bridge.

With the roles they were to play in the coming operation having been settled, the members of the team synchronized their watches and settled down to wait out the long, tense minutes and hours until the convoy's arrival.

Scully and Mockler were in the guardhouse, Findlay was crouched in the shadows near the detonator, and Lafcadio paced across the bridge in the manner of a Japanese sentry on perimeter patrol.

SERGEANT KONDO ROUSED his men from their slumber on the mossy ground of the jungle floor. He had heard the distinct sound of gunfire, and the reports had not come from a great distance away.

He called for the private who served as his aide to quickly fetch the sector map, then he spread the map on the ground before him. Kondo saw at once the answer to the question that had puzzled him and his deceased commander, Lieutenant Nakashimu.

At last Sergeant Kondo grasped the true nature of the objective which the American soldiers had been sent in to deal with. It was the bridge! All along it had been the bridge! What a fool he had been. What fools they had all been!

But now Kondo knew what he had to do. His responsibility was to get to the bridge on the double. Once there, he had to stop the Americans before it was too late. He shook his head with regret. A radio was what they needed, but the unit had been damaged during the firefight with the American forces. No matter, his men could handle the job alone if they moved fast enough—and if the fickle gods of war were on their side.

DAWN CAME with dense ground fog and with the sound of giant river toads croaking among the reeds. The water flowed on quietly under the bridge, and slowly, in patches, the fog started to lift.

As the sun came up completely, staining the girders of the bridge with an eerie blood-red light, Scully consulted his watch.

The time was 0540 hours.

The convoy was scheduled to cross in only a little while.

"Keep your eyes peeled," he called to the Filipino, stepping out of the guardhouse, attired in Japanese uniform. Lafcadio waved back, also wearing enemy combat fatigues. He knew what was expected of him and was fully prepared to do what was needed.

The sun was hot, and soon it burned off the residual wisps of the dense dawn fog. By six o'clock the sky was a clear, intense blue, and visibility was excellent. At 0615 hours, the first glint of a windshield was detected by Lafcadio as the lead truck of the Japanese supply convoy rounded the bend in the switchback road leading up to the bridge. The next glimpse showed it with its engine groaning as it labored to climb a steep incline, its brakes squealing from repeated applications by the driver as the vehicle bumped and lumbered along the boulder-strewn and deeply rutted roadway.

"Take care! They are coming!" the Filipino called out to the guardhouse, then turned back to face the oncoming Japanese, adjusting the peaked cap on his head so that its visor screened his face from view.

Scully turned toward Mockler and flashed Findlay the high-sign from the guardhouse. He saw Findlay wave back from his position a few hundred yards away. Everything was ready, he knew. All the pieces were falling into place. Each man felt his throat constrict and his heart speed up. The moment of truth was close at hand.

The convoy's lead vehicle had come so close to Lafcadio that the Filipino could see the two men seated in its cab through the windshield caked by yellow-brown road dust.

"Come on," he called out to them in Japanese as he waved his hands vigorously. The lead truck had stopped short as it gained the final few hundred yards to the access point of the bridge.

In response to Lafcadio's signal, the driver started the truck rolling and the convoy proceeded again. The

Filipino waved once more, then turned and loped toward the sentry box at the other end of the bridge without appearing to hurry too much, like a man who wants to get out of the way of an oncoming vehicle.

Having reached the center of the bridge, Lafcadio turned again toward the convoy and waved the lead truck forward once more. It kept on coming at a steady pace, heedless of the danger that it was rolling into.

Apparently the Japanese were buying it, Scully thought to himself as he watched from his station by the guardhouse. "That's it, man—keep them coming." His knuckles tensed on the butt of the captured Japanese rifle he ported as he stepped out from the guardhouse and waved on the lead truck while Mockler moved behind him and raised the yellow-and-black-striped barricade to a vertical position.

Lafcadio had reached their stations, and the three men stood only a few yards ahead of the lead Japanese transport truck as it crossed onto the bridge from the road, its gears grinding and its tires thudding over the planks.

According to plan, the three GIs inched toward the sides of the guardhouse. In another few seconds they were to run hell-bent for leather toward the protection of boulders lying along the margins of the road a couple of yards from the guardhouse, because as soon as the lead truck came abreast of the guardhouse, Findlay was to blow the charges.

A few hundred yards away, from his place of concealment in the thickets in the heights above the river,
Findlay saw the lead truck trundling steadily toward
the guardhouse. In only a second or two, he would
detonate the bundles of TNT that he had placed.

He raised the plunger and held the top edges of the
metal bar in his fists, ready to push down hard and
generate an electrical spark that would race along the
concealed cables to detonate the many pounds of high
explosive that he had rigged beneath the bridge.

Just before Findlay bore down on the plunger, Sergeant Kondo and his men reached the clearing. In a
flash the sergeant saw the American kneeling over the
detonator and the truck moving slowly across the
bridge. Instantly he knew what was about to take
place.

Ripping a submachine gun from the hands of the
private standing at his side, the sergeant cut loose with
a savage volley of chattering autofire that stitched
Findlay across the back as he crouched above the detonator box. Already dead, Findlay fell forward across
the detonator. The weight of his body pushed down
the plunger, creating a spark that raced down the wires
at the speed of light, blowing the detonator caps on the
TNT bundles and setting the charges off.

With the booming sound of rolling thunder, the
charges blew.

A heartbeat before Findlay fell, Scully, Mockler and
Lafcadio heard the burst of automatic fire from the

heights. They dodged for cover, but already one of the men inside the convoy's lead truck threw open the door, jumped out, leveled his rifle and got off a 3-round burst that cut down Lafcadio as he jumped over the side of the bridge. Killed instantly, Lafcadio's bullet-riddled body tumbled to the rocky terrain in the defile below. It bounced, rolled, then lay at the bottom, lifeless and still as death beside the flowing waters of the river.

Running full tilt and both taking flying leaps just as a wall of fire raced up behind them, Scully and Mockler hit the ground almost simultaneously and rolled as far as they were able to. As they did, they could feel the intense heat of the flames produced by the explosion wash over them in a sheet of fire and smelled the sickening odor or their own singed hair and flesh.

All hell was breaking loose, but they knew that the bridge was blowing skyward in a fountain of pulverized concrete and flaming metal shards, useless to the Japanese who so desperately needed it. Even if Findlay's charges blew them both to hell along with the bridge and the Japanese, the two servicemen each felt that despite all odds they accomplished their job.

Hell did not claim them, though. When the echoes of the explosion died away and the debris that had been hurled high into the air began to rain back to earth again through clouds of acrid high-explosive smoke, Scully and Mockler realized to their amazement that they were still alive, and if not unmarked, then at least still whole.

Their faces smudged by dirt, their billed caps pulled low over their faces, the two American GIs in Japanese fatigues slipped away from ground zero in the pandemonium reigning in the aftermath of the explosion and were already miles away before any semblance of order was restored.

For once luck was on their side.

31

Jacek was tending the small truck garden that he had set up beside the rectory building of Father Benigno's church.

Long days in the sun had turned his flesh the color of beaten bronze. His lank, black hair was long, worn Filipino-fashion. In the native garments that the padre had acquired for him, Jacek could pass for a native Filipino unless he was scrutinized up close.

He looked up at the sun, then down at the flourishing plants. A resigned but peaceful smile played about his lips. He had let go of his youthful dreams of becoming a ballroom king, another Fred Astaire on the silver screen. His body and mind had mended under the soothing influence of the tropical sun, and he felt content to stay where he was. Here he was accepted without a second thought, and without being compared to the whole-bodied man he had been.

The roar of an engine caught his ears. He glanced up and saw a U.S. Army jeep emblazoned with the five-pointed star on its olive drab hood grinding its way up to the church. The driver stopped the jeep just outside the churchyard and climbed out of the cab. Then he walked briskly toward Jacek.

It didn't take Jacek long to recognize Matt Scully. Only now, Scully wore the bar of a second lieutenant on his sleeve, as well as the patch of the Sunshine Division. A Purple Heart nestled among other medals and ribbons of valor on the right side of his neat and crispy "A" uniform.

Jacek raised his hand to his head and smartly saluted the officer who was coming toward him. Stopping a few feet from the jeep he'd just left, Scully saluted back.

"At ease, soldier," he said in his familiar gravelly voice.

"Permission to speak, sir," Jacek replied.

"Permission granted, Private."

"Just because they gave you a promotion, sir," Jacek said with a lopsided smile, "don't mean you ain't as pug-ugly as you were when you were a sergeant, *sir,*" he told Scully.

"No," Scully admitted. "But the dames go for the uniform. That's what counts." A moment later the two reunited soldiers of Third Platoon were shaking hands and slapping each other's back, in the manner of men who had long ago given one another up for dead. Then they moved indoors in search of Father Benigno.

They found him lighting votive candles in a little alcove located near the entrance to the chapel. Scully produced a pocket flask of Scotch. Then the padre brought out three glasses and Scully poured them two fingers each.

The three of them had a drink while sitting around a small table in the father's office, and Scully filled Jacek in on what had happened to the unit.

"All of 'em got it, Sarge," Jacek repeated, shaking his head when Scully had finished, not able to believe that what he had heard was true.

"All except for Mockler, yeah," Scully intoned with finality. "And *you,* my friend. Which brings me to the point of why I'm here. Until you get your discharge put in, your soul might belong to God but your ass still belongs to Uncle Sam.

"I'm here to see that Uncle Sam gets you back. After I pour you both another round, say your good-byes to the padre and pack your gear. You're coming with me."

"Comin' where, Sarge?" Jacek asked. "There's nothing for me back home. Not with only one leg, there isn't."

Scully pulled a thin V-Mail letter from his shirt pocket and slid it across the table toward Jacek. "Smells like perfume," he said with a grin. "Must be from a secret admirer."

Jacek unsealed the V-Mail envelope and curiously scanned the letter. He hadn't seen mail from home in a hell of a long time. In a couple of minutes he looked up. His face wore a stunned expression. He looked like a man who had been clubbed squarely on the head.

"It's from Annabell," he shouted at Scully and Father Benigno. "She says I'm a father! You hear that!

I'm a father!'' Jacek repeated. "I got a little girl back home!"

"That calls for a toast," Scully said. He poured them all another slug of Scotch and raised his glass high in a toast to Jacek's good luck.

Father Benigno drained his glass quickly, set it down with a crash and ran for the belfry as fast as his legs could carry him. Scully and Jacek traded questioning glances as they saw him sprint from the room, wondering if the padre had suddenly gone mad.

A few minutes later the joyful ringing of church bells echoed through the hill country of Luzon.

**Now you can get your copies of
the first two volumes of
the hard-hitting miniseries...**

by William Reed

In Book 1: BLOOD AND GLORY, the tall Texans are bound for trouble when their National Guard unit faces the onslaught of the Nazi juggernaut.

In Book 2: COMPANY OF HEROES, the focus is on Dog Company—the fiercest unit of the Thunderbirds of Oklahoma—as they face tough odds to save the Allied effort.

Bolan is no stranger to the hellfire trail.

DON PENDLETON's
MACK BOLAN®
HARDLINE

Corrupt electronics tycoons are out to make a killing by selling
ultrasecret military hardware to anyone with the cash. One of
their targets is a man with one foot in the grave, an occult-
obsessed defense contractor.

Mack Bolan finds himself enmeshed in a mission that grows
more bizarre by the minute, involving spirits and Stealth,
mystics and murderers.

Go for a hair-raising ride in

JAMES AXLER

DEATH LANDS

Dark Carnival

Trapped in an evil baron's playground, the rides are downhill and dangerous for Ryan Cawdor and his roving band of warrior-survivalists.

For one brief moment after their narrow escape, Ryan thinks they have found the peace and idyll they so desperately seek. But a dying messenger delivers a dark message....